JUST FOR YOU

JENNIFER ANN SHORE

Print ISBN: 979-8-9859928-0-9

*For Morgan Blank,
my first Seattle friend,
who left me for sunshine
but shared her hockey love*

ONE

Breakfast is a full-contact sport.

I wish that wasn't the case, but it's been that way for as long as I can remember.

I'm a morning person. I usually rise before my alarm, and I have no problem shrugging off any pulls of sleep once I'm awake.

If I had it my way, I'd spend each day enjoying a nice, quiet meal before school. Maybe in another life I'd become some sort of worldly individual, reading up on current events on my phone or even unfolding the newspaper my mom still has delivered each morning.

But instead, I merely wait for the impending chaos.

Our kitchen isn't exactly small, but the number of people in it at one time—me, my mom, my stepdad, and my four half-siblings—can be overwhelming.

It's almost surprising the bathroom isn't the most congested place in the house, but my mom worked out a schedule years ago that we've all adhered to without issue. It also helps that we're all on slightly different wake-up times and that I've set up a tiny desk in the corner of my room where I do most of my primping.

So while we move through that high-traffic area with ease, having removed one hurdle in the getting-ready process, I swear it only pushes all the disarray down to the kitchen.

I turn off my straightener and double-check my appearance—too long limbs, slightly frizzy hair, same brown eyes as my mother—in the full-length mirror that's tacked up in my closet, then I bound down the stairs.

Thankfully, I'm the first one here this morning, so I get first pick from the available breakfast foods.

I hear the pitter-patter of my family members milling about on the floor above, and it fuels my urgency as I open the pantry.

I've tried to keep everything organized, but no matter what system I implement, it's always a disaster within hours. The shelves are overstuffed with various snack bags and canned and boxed dry goods, but I shove everything out of my way as I search for the grand prize.

When I come up empty, I blink in confusion, wondering if I've somehow managed to hide the container from *myself*. I move a box of granola bars three times, as if that will magically make what I'm looking for jump out and surprise me.

"Good morning, Violet," my mom says cheerfully as she enters the kitchen and immediately opens the fridge.

I pull back, flicking the cereal boxes in annoyance as I turn to face her.

She's dressed for the day in jeans and a casual gray t-shirt, which she'll "fancy up," as she likes to say, with a blazer before she heads into work. Her strawberry blonde hair is twirled up in rollers on the top of her head—though they all threaten to topple over as she moves around the kitchen.

"Mom," I say, letting my annoyance come through in that one syllable.

She quirks an eyebrow at me as she presses the button on the coffee maker. "What?"

"Have you seen the last of the chocolate banana muffins I made?"

I don't mention that I went to bed thinking about warming those two perfect pastries in the toaster oven before slathering a massive glob of butter over every bit of them.

Really, the best motivation for getting out of bed—or doing anything in life—is food.

But as her expression morphs into something slightly sheepish, I know that my dreams are going to be dashed.

"I just assumed you already hid away whatever you wanted."

"I did," I admit before sinking my teeth into my bottom lip.

"Well, I didn't know it was the last of them," she says, tapping the counter with her nails. "Are you sure you don't have another batch somewhere else?"

"I did that with those almond-crusted fig cookies *one time*," I argue.

"Maybe the container just got moved around," she says with determination.

She takes it upon herself to conduct a repeat of the search I did, but no amount of pantry Jenga is going to make the delicious pastries appear where I last saw them.

I let out a massive sigh as she frowns at the shelves, coming to the same conclusion I did.

Those beautiful muffins—that are really more suited for dessert than breakfast—are gone.

"I'm so sorry, Violet," she says after a few minutes. "I should have known that anything behind the Frosted Flakes and the cans of lentil soup was off-limits."

"Yeah."

"When Chloe asked if she could have some, I thought—"

I groan. "You let *Chloe* have them?"

She pulls out the coffee pot, pours a splash into her mug, and then fills the remaining space with milk. "You know they're her favorite."

"Boundaries, Mom," I remind her. "You promised."

It's a discussion I've had many times with her and Ryan, but there's been only minimal change in behavior from her —and my siblings.

"I know," she tells me. "I'm sorry. I'm trying, really, but you can't blame me for not having a mental inventory of our pantry and your baking projects."

I don't offer her any words, just a curt nod as I busy myself with toasting a plain and very boring bagel, which is not only store-bought but a day past its expiration.

And even worse, it's not until I've got both halves on my plate that I realize we're out of cream cheese.

When I finally have it coated with the final dregs from

the peanut butter jar and slightly congealed fig jam, I sit down at the table.

I take the first bite, and, unfortunately for me, the sound of my chewing doesn't overpower the roar of my siblings coming down the stairs, likely all in different states of dress and wakefulness.

I'm the oldest of the five of us by a number of years, which means that while I'm the least of my mother's worries, I'm also the biggest thorn in her side most of the time.

I don't have many memories of when it was just the two of us, and I don't have any at all from when she and my biological father were together. They got pregnant while dating in college, and after graduating, they went their separate ways—and he's been a very sporadic presence ever since.

My mom likes to gloss over the details of how hard it was, but it must have been so lonely and awful for her. I mean, she was stuck with a colicky baby while my biological father took his dream job in the Middle East—and my grandparents cut her off for having a baby out of wedlock.

I roll my eyes at the thought of just how outdated their thinking was, but they both died before I was old enough to come to that opinion and tell them so.

My mother met Ryan by chance when I was five years old. I was, apparently, screaming my head off in the middle of the grocery store because I'd lost my stuffed penguin, and Ryan chased us into the parking lot to return it.

They had an instant connection—or so I've been told—and I definitely take credit for their meet-cute.

I glance up at the photo framed on the wall, which was snapped by a stranger on a disposable camera at their courthouse wedding. They're posing at the altar while I sleep in Ryan's arms, and they both look ridiculously happy.

Even though we're not genetically related, Ryan is the best father figure I could have ever hoped for—and I love him enough to forgive the fact that he is partially responsible for the terror I undergo before eight o'clock every morning.

"Mom!" June, the oldest of my younger siblings, yells as she runs down the hallway.

"June," my mom returns. "Inside voice, please."

"Right." June slides across the floor in her socks, waving her arms like a bird until she comes to a stop. "I can't find my green shirt."

My mom gives me an exasperated look over the rim of her coffee cup, and it's relatable enough that I momentarily forget I'm mad at her for the state of my breakfast.

"What's wrong with the one you have on?" she asks June.

I tilt my head at my sister who immediately backs away as I stare her down. "That's my favorite shirt," I accuse.

My mom frowns at her. "Is that true?"

"Well, in my defense, I can't find my green shirt," June whines. "And this one was the closest to it."

"It's yellow," I say flatly.

"You were the one who taught me about the color wheel," she retorts.

It's true.

But it happened when I was explaining to her that I use

purple food coloring to turn buttercream white, not about anything clothing-related.

"I wanted to match Courtney and Sophia today." June gives my mom a pleading look. "We planned it out and everything and now I'm going to be the only one who looks different!"

I sigh at her dramatics, less in the mood to hear her drag this out than get my shirt back.

"I'll give you a pass today," I say. "But the next time I find out that you've gone into my closet without asking, I'm going to make you change immediately. I don't care if you and your fourth-grade minions are in the middle of the playground at the moment and you don't have anything to change into. Streak at school for all I care."

My mom scolds me with a shake of her head. "Violet."

"Got it?" I press to June.

"Got it," she agrees with a grumble.

My mom leans on the counter to start her campaign of consoling June, assuring her that she looks fine, even if it's not the right color, and I roll my eyes before I take another bite.

As I swallow, the twins—Chloe and Kevin—bound into the kitchen and head straight for me like missiles. I jump up and hold my plate aloft before they can get their grubby little fingers all over it.

"Absolutely not, you two," I snap.

I move back toward my mother, intending to use her as a wall of defense if I need to.

Chloe, the taller of the two, makes a play for my plate while Kevin puts all his weight on my feet to try and hold me in place.

"Don't break anything," my mom warns.

"That's your main concern?" I scowl.

She hides her smile by taking another sip of coffee. "We're already down a full place setting from dinner last week."

"Not cool," I say to my siblings.

But they carry on, trying to drag me down as I move.

I shove the rest of my bagel in my mouth, which isn't an easy feat, and push them both off me as I drop the plate in the dishwasher.

Even without the possibility of stealing my food, the twins don't give up, working to take me down to the ground, apparently just for the sake of it.

I can't help but laugh at their lack of strength, but my triumphant expression evaporates as four-year-old Brandon, who we all still affectionately refer to as "The Baby," comes out of nowhere to knock into my knees.

I tumble down to the ground, eliciting victorious cries from all of them.

"Agh!" I yell as The Baby falls on my chest.

He wraps his arms around me and rubs his snotty nose on my arm. "Violet," he drawls.

"So gross," I groan as I shove him off. "Mom, come on."

"Okay, that's enough," my mother says sharply. "Sit at the table and eat your breakfast like civilized humans, or go up to your room until I'm ready to leave."

Her tone is stern enough that they comply instantly.

Of her and Ryan, she's not usually the one to play hardball.

It's usually only at my request because she finds the

antics endearing—I think she'd be more on my side if she wasn't an only child and experienced what I do every single day. To my siblings, I'm a cross between a friend, parent, and jungle gym, and I don't love it.

Thankfully, though, at her word, all my siblings walk toward the table in a comically straight line that looks like some sort of military formation.

My mother sets a bowl of cereal in front of each of them —Cocoa Puffs for June, Lucky Charms for the twins, Cheerios for The Baby—and I gratefully accept a glass of orange juice from her.

When her back is turned, I grab a few of the still-dry marshmallows from Chloe's bowl for myself. The little sugary red balloons and blue moons are like little bits of serotonin. I definitely wish I was having my chocolate banana muffins instead, but I'll accept this as measly payback.

"Hey," Chloe cries.

I swallow the evidence before she can rat me out, then wink at her.

She glares and sticks her tongue out, then fixes her face back to normal as her dad crosses the threshold.

"Well, well, well, if it isn't all my favorite humans in one place," Ryan says.

That line is ridiculously cheesy, but I can't help but grin like an idiot every time he says something like that.

"You look nice," my mom says as she hands him a fresh cup of coffee.

He straightens his tie before he drops a kiss on my mom's cheek. "Thank you."

"Ready for the big presentation today?"

"Ready as I'll ever be," he says with a smile.

"What's it for?" I ask.

"You remember my boss?" Ryan pauses until I nod. "It's her, along with *her* boss and a few people on the finance team you met as we walked out of the building. Going over some early projections for this quarter and doing some planning for next year."

"Cool," I say, instantly connecting faces and the setup of his office in my mind.

Ryan brought me along for last year's Bring the Kids to Work Day, and while I thought it would be really boring, it was actually kind of cool.

He does event marketing for a plastics company. I didn't really understand what it meant until I saw him in action, making networking calls, leading meetings, approving new graphic designs, and leading negotiations with trade show vendors. I guess it all sounds kind of lame on a surface level, but it was nice to see how passionate he is about his work.

Since then, he's made it a point to bring me little samples from the shop floor and trinkets from his conferences, and I've appreciated his effort to include me in the conversations.

My mom, on the other hand, works as a bookkeeper and assistant manager for a local bookstore and cafe called Books & Beans.

I've done an absolutely terrible job of taking advantage of her employee discount, but June has stacks of books that are all meticulously organized by genre and author last name.

"Everyone get some good sleep last night?" Ryan asks.

"Yes," my siblings reply in chorus.

He makes a point to not sit down until my mother does, waving for her to take her spot and stop fussing around the kitchen. She finally joins us, and he squeezes her shoulder before he takes his seat at the head of the table.

"June was snoring so loud last night," Chloe says, grinning devilishly.

"Was not," June protests. "I don't snore."

"I was awake, not you," Chloe retorts. "I heard it!"

I don't mention that I can often hear June's snoring through the shared wall that separates my room from theirs because I don't want to get dragged into the bickering.

June slurps the last of her sugary milk on her spoon. "I don't believe you."

Ryan tilts his head, assessing his daughter. "Isn't that Violet's shirt?"

June's entire demeanor slumps under the weight of the continued scrutiny. "I already said I was sorry."

Ryan nudges me with his elbow, knowing that just one word from me will instantly lift my sister's spirits.

I don't know if familial relation means I'm compelled to take care of my brothers and sisters even when they're frustrating me, but after Ryan's silent encouragement, the feeling surfaces more than I want it to.

I clear my throat. "I actually think it looks better on her than it does on me."

June startles, appearing genuinely shocked to hear my praise, and the smile that forms almost splits her face in half. "You really think so?"

I nod as I get up and put my glass in the top rack of the dishwasher. "It's much better suited with your hair now, anyway."

Ryan beams like he's proud of my maturity and graciousness, but I merely shrug in his direction.

"Well," June says after a beat. "Sophia *did* say that I have the coolest hair in the class."

"You do," I agree, stepping over to ruffle her locks, which are a distinct shade of purple.

Last Saturday, my mom and Ryan took my other siblings to a birthday party for one of the twins' classmates, and June and I stayed behind for a little girls' night. We took turns painting each other's nails and doing face masks before ending the night dyeing our hair new colors—something my mom approved before she left.

June very sweetly chose a shade of violet, while I slathered my blonde hair with an orangey red color that she says reminds her of the sunset.

"Mom," Chloe whines. "I want to dye my hair next."

My mother chuckles and shakes her head. "Let's work on keeping your side of the room clean first, okay? Show us that you can handle responsibility before we start letting you do big girl things."

Chloe merely huffs in response.

Kevin and The Baby are totally uninterested in the conversation around them, being more invested in pretending to shoot at each other across the table with their spoons.

And I need to get out of here before I become their next target.

I take my keys off the hook and grab my backpack from its spot by the garage door. "I'll see you later."

"Have a good day, sweetheart," my mom says.

Ryan tilts his travel mug toward me in *cheers* motion.

And I actually let out a smile as I leave the kitchen—and breakfast—behind.

TWO

After the mayhem during my first meal of the day, it's nice that I can count on lunch to be predictable.

It's been almost the exact same routine for the past four years—we sit at the same table, surrounded by the same assortment of classmates and friends, while eating the same rotation of meals scooped on plastic trays.

Marshall High School is a perfectly average public school that, at the very least, is a safe haven where I don't have to concern myself with nagging siblings and my stuff getting stolen.

Well, kind of...

"Hey, did you do that math homework?" Erica catches up with me, like usual, just as I've stepped into the cafeteria.

Her question is one I have gotten at least two dozen times this year alone.

It's a good thing that Erica's and my strengths balance out—she struggles in math and whatever science class we're taking but makes up for my inadequacies in English and broadcast journalism, which is my only elective this year.

Senioritis is getting the best of us both, though, and with our college applications all sent in and no news coming to us until the spring, there's not much to do other than coast by and enjoy our last moments together while we wait for the inevitable.

But she's been slacking much more than I have, resulting in the same exchange almost every day.

"Violet," she repeats, tucking a lock of her chin-length black hair behind her ear. "Math homework?"

"Yes, I did it." I raise an eyebrow, waiting for the question that's sure to follow.

She grins in return. "Can I copy it?"

We both already know that I'm going to hand it over the moment we sit down at our table, which is why after we grab our trays of sandwiches and salads and get situated, Erica holds out her hand.

I relent easily, pulling my worksheet out of its folder in my bag and sliding it across to her.

If it were anyone else, I might actually get annoyed by how expectant she is.

But Erica is one of my two best friends in the world, so I give her some leeway. If Kara, my other best friend, was here instead of the school she transferred to three years ago, she'd be huffing on my behalf.

I've known them both forever—the three of us were in the same daycare as kids. Our moms were always late in picking us up, which happened enough times that the providers suggested we work out some sort of carpooling schedule.

And it all happened from there.

We managed to stay close even when Kara's parents moved her out of the district at the start of sophomore year. Well, Kara and I have—it's a different story with her and Erica.

I didn't notice any sort of tension between them until after the move happened. Without the buffer of class and assignments to talk about, I assumed they were just slowly growing apart and finding different interests.

I was always the one who initiated plans between the three of us, determined to keep our little Three Musketeers vibe going.

It all came to a head at a sleepover last year. I popped downstairs to plate a batch of freshly baked brownies for us, and when I came back up to my room, I could tell something was off.

Neither of them said a word directly to each other for the rest of the night—or have since fessed up to me what the issue is—and Erica left before Kara or I even woke up the next morning.

But they've refused to be in the same room since.

I've been stuck in the middle, trying to placate them both by sharing my time and attention, which is far more difficult with Kara since she's busy with her practice schedule and doesn't live that close by.

Our dynamic is like that of a child and their divorced parents—awkward, tense, and full of unanswered questions —which I'm, thankfully, spared from in my actual family.

"Are you sure number five is right?" Erica asks suddenly.

Her tone is a little too impatient considering I'm saving her from getting a zero on the assignment, and I don't exactly appreciate it.

I suppose I'm on edge from getting tackled in the kitchen this morning, so I let out a sigh to relieve some of my inner tension, then glance up at her in the midst of stabbing my ranch-covered salad with a fork.

"Yes," I say confidently. "Do you want me to explain it?"

She squints at the problem in front of her like it's going to help her understand it. "No."

"Hey, hey," Emily says as she and Aksa join us. "God, today has *sucked.*"

"Why?" Erica asks, not even looking up from the assignment. "Did Mr. Davis not 'see the vision' in your art project that you hastily put together in the parking lot this morning?"

"Someone's feeling mean today," Emily says with an eyeroll.

"No, I'm just direct and *concentrating,*" Erica retorts.

Emily's unbothered by her sharpness at this point, accustomed to this behavior during our lunchtime rituals but also because we've been spending more time together this year in our broadcast journalism class.

It's funny how your social groups can be totally transformed by mere proximity.

Aksa, like me, prefers numbers and equations over the humanities classes at our school. But in a pivot from my personality, she actually enjoys being on camera.

She and Erica co-anchor the weekly news broadcast,

taking turns reading stories as they lead the half-hour show with banter and poise. They're a good duo, and their strong chemistry makes the show somewhat entertaining.

Emily, in turn, spends most of her time "fact-checking" and flirting with the guy who runs the sports desk, and he seems to eat up the attention.

I absolutely refuse to do anything but be in the background, and with no technical skills in that area to speak of, I'm relegated to doing the "weather," which I actually really love. I get to stare at all the apps on my phone, studying the temperatures, precipitation formations, and trends, then put together a little graphic every Monday before I work on other homework during class time.

It's interesting and productive, and it's also an easy A.

"And in tonight's breaking news, Erica Song, lead anchor of the weekly news program and president and likely *only* member of the improv club, is once again saved from failing calculus," Aksa says, putting on her best news anchor voice.

I don't bother hiding my laugh. "It's kind of scary how easily you can slip into that personality."

"She learned from the best," Erica says flippantly.

"Are you referring to yourself?" Aksa clarifies. "Because I haven't learned *anything* from you other than how to take advantage of the goodwill of your friends."

"Shut up," Erica grumbles, fighting to not let the corners of her mouth tick upward.

"See, I have all my homework done *and* my news package ready for next week," Aksa continues, ignoring her completely. "The librarian was thrilled that I was interested in doing a segment on the new layout of the shelves, which helps clarify confusion. She was so happy that she gave me a stack of passes to get out of class to collect b-roll and whatever else I need for the story."

Erica sighs as she scribbles down the last answer on her worksheet. "That's unethical."

"That's genius, actually," Emily says as her eyes light up. "What do I have to do to get one of those?"

Aksa considers it as she chews on a french fry. "Help me convince Violet to bring us gingerbread cookies on Monday."

"The butterscotch ones?" Emily asks.

Aksa smiles. "Yep."

I groan at the thought of what a pain that dough is to work with. "Again? I've already made two batches of them for you guys *this month*. I could try out something else? Maybe just plain butterscotch—"

"You can't mess with perfection," Aksa insists, shaking her head. "Besides, it's the most delicious combination for fall."

"It's a whole vibe," Emily agrees, dramatically wiggling her perfectly groomed eyebrows. "Like a real-life Pinterest board. Scarves. Hot tea. Butterscotch gingerbread cookies."

"For what it's worth, I would enjoy that, too," Erica says, sliding my homework back to me.

I *feel* the weight of their three stares as I focus solely on putting my worksheet away.

"Fine," I relent, drawing out the syllable.

They all let out a cheer, then immediately start chatting about how excited they are to exist in this season, which is punctuated by the oohs and aahs over Emily's new thigh-high boots.

It's a nice feeling of camaraderie, but an errant thought in the back of my mind threatens to become a legitimate concern...

Just like I can count on Erica to ask me for homework, Aksa to be snarky, and Emily to check her appearance in her phone reflection at least three times a period, I wonder if part of *their* routine is me being a pushover.

And I don't like that one bit.

"But I want one of those hall passes, too," I interrupt.

I don't actually have a need for it or even a real desire to slink out of class at will—I say it merely to assuage my own inner panic.

"Done," Aksa says with a smirk before reaching into her bag and handing one over.

I nod as I accept it and place it in my bag, feeling marginally better already.

I run through my mental list of ingredients that we definitely have in the cabinets at home, knowing that tonight I'll have to take stock of what's low or out. And I'll need to work out a better hiding place because I'm pretty sure Chloe ate all the butterscotch last—

"What are you lovely ladies chatting about?"

The deep sound of Alex's voice interrupts my thoughts, and I withhold all emotion as he slides in beside Erica and puts his arm around her shoulders.

If there's one bonus to his presence, it's that everything else falls out of my brain, clearing my mind of all doubt, even if it's replaced by annoyance with his arrival.

I see the same feelings mirrored in Aksa's expression with her brows pinched and mouth pressed in a flat line, but Emily looks at Alex and Erica like she's watching her favorite romance movie play out in real time.

"Hi, Alex," she says a little dreamily.

Even worse, Erica looks at her boyfriend like he's some sort of deity gracing us all with his presence, overtaking everything else in her life.

I have one guess as to what's distracting her from her homework, and he's six feet tall.

"Violet's going to bring us all treats on Monday," Erica explains. "Her butterscotch gingerbread cookies."

His eyes light up as they meet mine. "Awesome. Those are my favorite."

I force a smile. "That's good."

I don't mention that I don't make them for *him* because my body has an internal and involuntary reaction to his direct gaze.

It's almost disarming how aggressively attractive he is.

And he definitely uses it to his advantage.

He's got a bright white smile, a set of deep blue eyes, slightly mussed-up brown hair, and a sort of *charm* that I can't quantify with anything other than being excessively likable to most people.

But there's something about him that I honestly can't stand, and it's been this way even before he and Erica started dating last year.

Despite the fact that everyone loves him, he seems to spare no mind for their feelings, only his amusement. He's the kind of guy who will make fun of someone while having his arm around their shoulders, acting as if they're in on the joke instead of the butt of it.

And I can remember one really uncomfortable geography class last year when he pretended to not speak English just to mess with the very young and nervous substitute teacher, which was problematic on so many levels.

Alex rubs his hands together and awards me with another smile. "Are we placing orders, or is the menu already decided?"

"Decided," Aksa says, cutting him off.

I'm grateful for it because Erica would have likely enabled his entitlement and volunteered even more of my time.

"Maybe on the next round," Erica adds, keeping the peace. "You know Violet's always in the kitchen, testing different flours and comparing baking soda to baking powder and that sort of thing."

"I consider it a perk to our relationship," Alex teases as he helps himself to Erica's lunch. "A third wheel who brings us baked goods."

Erica howls at his attempt at a joke.

Aksa wrinkles her nose and physically turns away from him as she pivots the conversation. "So, what's everyone up to this weekend?"

"My mom's making me do yard work." Emily lets out an exaggerated sigh as she examines her nails. "We have to 'winterize' everything. Like move the patio furniture into the garage and rake leaves and stuff."

"That sucks," Erica says.

"It does," Emily agrees. "What about you?"

Erica smiles up at Alex before she leans on his arm. "We have big plans to celebrate our six-month anniversary."

"Oh my gosh!" Emily lets out a little squeal. "Already? That's so exciting! What are you doing?"

"He won't tell me." Erica looks at Alex with adoration, lips in a pout and eyelashes batting. "It's a surprise."

"Will you tell me?" Emily asks him conspiratorially.

"My lips are sealed," Alex says before he smiles. "Well, kind of."

He then drops a kiss on the top of Erica's head and mumbles something in her ear that I, thankfully, can't hear.

"I've got plans with my cousin to go to the movies and not much else," Aksa says. "What about you, Violet? More hair-dyeing escapades with June?"

I laugh and tug at the ends of my hair. "I think I'll keep this color for now. But, uh, I'm going to a hockey game tonight. Kara's big varsity debut over at Greene."

Erica's eyes narrow, but Alex perks up and leans with his elbows on the table.

"*You* are going to a hockey game?" he scoffs.

"Uh-huh," I breathe.

"You're going to go see and support a rival team before you come to one of *my* games?" Alex holds his hand to his heart like I've stabbed him. "I don't know whether to be devastated or offended."

"Neither, please," I say flatly. "No need to go to extremes."

"That's so exciting, though," Aksa says with a smile. "She's finally made it, then?"

"Yeah," I say, pride swelling as I think about all Kara has gone through.

"What's the big deal?" Emily asks as she opens a crinkly bag of chips.

"Kara has been trying to play on the hockey team at her school for years, but they only allow boys to join," I explain. "She fought a few rounds with the coaches and the parents of other players, and finally, Kara and her parents got the school board to change the rules. Even after they got it done, the coaches made her go through a set of really tough tryouts. But she made it. Obviously. No one was really surprised. But her first official game is tonight."

Alex stretches his arms up, totally unbothered and unimpressed. "I can't imagine a girl playing on our team."

"Because you're sexist?" I retort.

Aksa snorts into her Diet Coke while Emily looks confused and Erica lets out an awkward guffaw.

"W-what?" Alex sputters before grinning widely in an attempt to act like my accusation is a joke. "Of course not."

"Yeah," Erica backs him up as he laughs it off. "Of course not."

Alex shakes his head. "It's for your own protection, really. I mean, have you ever been to a hockey game?"

"Yes, of course," I say immediately.

But I definitely don't cop to the fact that I spend most of the time chewing my nails and willing the other players to not send a puck directly into Kara's face.

"It's brutal," he says seriously. "I mean, I guess watching from behind the glass is fine, but actually play-ing? You're, like, the most quiet and risk-averse person I know, Vi. You'd get crushed in a second."

"I would," I admit, trying to keep the venom out of my voice. "Because I'm not Kara, who has been training and playing her entire life."

Alex shrugs at my counterargument, but he backs off.

There's an awkward beat of silence where I continue to glare at him, but Erica clears her throat and breaks it.

"So, Alex, did you hear about…"

Even though the subject is changed, I immediately tune out their voices.

Because I've just come to the realization that one of my best friends is enabling the very behavior the other is trying to overcome—and I don't know what this says about me as a person who loves both equally.

THREE

In all the years I've spent watching Kara's games, I have yet to figure out what I find so appealing about being at the ice rink.

The moment I step inside I'm hit with a singular blast of artificial heat—even though it's not that cold out yet for November—that is gone the moment I move away from the vent.

I know better than to remove my jacket because, even though there's a scuffed-up wall and a protective plexiglass barrier around the ice, it's still chilly in the metal bleachers.

I grab a cup of hot chocolate before I hit the stands, appreciating the simplicity of artificially flavored chocolate powder that somehow becomes liquid gold.

There's a small crowd here for Greene's first game of the season, which is a surprisingly good turnout. I scan the faces knowing I won't see anyone familiar—Kara's mom is home sick, and her dad has a shift at the hospital tonight.

Hockey isn't the most popular sport in my town or Kara's, getting trumped by soccer and track, but it's my favorite.

I'm a little reluctant to admit it because it's not the sport itself that I appreciate. I like watching the players fly around on their skates as they warm up and hearing the strange echo of cheering and the sticks slapping against one another.

And, oddly enough, the scent I associate with this entire endeavor heightens the experience.

I like the smell of gasoline because of the chemical reaction it sparks in my brain and chlorine because of the nostalgia that comes from summers at the pool, but I can't put my finger on exactly why I like being around the ice rink.

It's a mix of sweat, sulfur, and buttery popcorn, which seems like a disgusting combination—but I find it comforting.

Alluring, even.

I smile as the two teams break their huddles and get into position on the ice.

From my vantage point, it's hard to see Kara's game face. She's covered in gear from head to toe, and the extra protection afforded to the goalie means it's even more difficult to make her out.

She joked a while ago that she didn't understand why it was such a big deal to let her play on the boys' team because if she just showed up with a mask on and her hair stuffed into her helmet, no one would ever know.

I disagreed with that sentiment, though—she's so good

that *of course* she would stand out regardless of what team she's on.

The buzzer sounds as the puck is dropped on the ice, officially signaling the start of the game, and the chaos begins.

I've picked up enough over the years—from watching games, listening to Kara talk through strategy, and reading about her in articles—to understand the level of coordination and athleticism this sport requires, and I try my best to appreciate it.

The players zoom across the ice, and it's so fast and cutthroat that sometimes I can barely keep up.

The sensation reminds me of when June wanted to pretend she was a magician a few weeks ago. Her only trick was putting a ball under three cups and moving them around quickly, and I got a headache from trying to keep my gaze on the correct one.

But unlike my sister's short-lived stunt, I've had nearly a decade to acclimate to hockey, along with Kara's training schedule and incessant habit of bouncing a tennis ball, which she claims is good for her hand dexterity.

Thankfully, the action for the first third of the game is predominantly on the other end of the ice, which is good for Kara's team and my nerves.

I spend most of that time watching her move around the net, noticing how her long blonde hair is braided out of the way, only partially obscuring the name on the back of her jersey.

She shakes out her limbs, and though they're well-protected under her blockers, pads, and gloves, I don't exactly *enjoy* that someone I love dearly is putting herself in harm's way.

But no matter how battered and bruised she gets from the sport, she's happy, and that's all that matters to me.

I take a sip of my lukewarm drink, noting it's been long enough since I bought it that the marshmallows have melted into a congealed barrier. I try to suck them through the lip in the lid, but I merely end up with a very sticky mouth.

In the third period, I start to get a little antsy because the other team picks up their aggression, trying to make up for the two goals Kara's team has already scored.

The defense holds strong, and so does she—clearing away the one shot that comes through with swift and decisive accuracy that earns a gasp from the crowd.

Normally during these games, I do homework or look at the weather forecasts in parts of the world I've never been to, but I feel like since this is such a big deal for her, I should give a concentrated effort of moral support.

It's somewhat of a struggle, especially as the players become blurs, and I get distracted by the commentary of the people around me.

But eventually, the final buzzer sounds, jarring me back.

I blink as people begin to trickle out of the stands instead of sticking around to watch the lineup of handshakes or wait for the players to be released for the night.

I suppose for most of the people here this game is just like any other season opener that ended in the team's favor.

But not for me.

And certainly not for Kara, who I can't wait to hug in celebration.

Taking small steps, I slowly follow the crowd out, knowing Kara won't be available right away. There will likely be some post-game recap from the coaches and time spent getting cleaned up, but I'm fine to wait for her.

The ice resurfacer makes its appearance to smooth the rink, creating those satisfying clean lines for the public skate that's open for the next hour. I've never partaken myself, but it's funny to see the little kids ready for an exciting Friday night of wiping out on the ice.

I head toward the lobby, inhaling the scent of rubber and whatever artificial cleaner they use to disinfect the ice skates between renters, then come to a stop at a flat wooden bench in front of where I think Kara will exit.

I drop onto it and watch as a couple gets drinks from the concession stand. Their order spurs me to think about how I can create some sort of hot chocolate dessert without making it s'mores flavored.

Not that there's anything wrong with delicious chocolate, marshmallow, and graham cracker vibes, but to me, that's a summer treat, and I want something that fits the impending winter.

Maybe if I add little sprinkles of peppermint or some sort of nut it would—

My line of thinking is cut off when the locker room door opens with such force that it slams against the white stone walls.

I jump up as the players step out with grins on their faces and equipment bags slung over their shoulders. A few of them eye me with interest, but I keep my gaze fixed as I wait for Kara to make an appearance.

She doesn't, though, and I let out a sigh.

"You okay?"

I turn at the voice, expecting an employee or manager of the ice rink to see if I need help with something, but I get one of Kara's teammates.

It's hard to see who any of the players are under their helmets and full-face cages during the game, but now, I get to connect this guy's face with his jersey—number eleven —which is strung over his bag. I recall seeing him line up in the middle of the ice in the center position, but other than that, I don't have any details or even his name.

As I meet his curious dark brown eyes, I realize I've left him hanging.

"Yeah," I say quickly. "I'm fine."

He tilts his head like he's waiting for me to elaborate.

"Thanks for asking, though," I add.

A piece of his chin-length brown hair lands on the side of his smirk. "Are you…waiting for someone?"

"Uh, yeah."

"Cool," he says with a nod.

I wring my hands, hating how awkward and uncertain his presence is making me. "Do you need something?" I ask.

My question is a little direct and rude, but I don't think I've ever met this guy before, and I definitely don't know what he wants from me.

The door opens again, and the clanging causes my heart to lurch in hope that it's Kara, but it's just more of her teammates.

A hulking redhead eyes the two of us as he walks by. "You coming, Penn?"

I immediately recall the significance of *that* name and then look at the guy in front of me with newfound respect.

He accepts a pat on the back before he waves them off. "I'll meet you guys there."

"Don't take too long," his teammate calls back. "We cleaned out the diner's entire display case in, like, twenty minutes last time, remember?"

Penn chuckles, and creases form around his eyes, etching his delight in his features. "I'll never forget that."

I shift on my feet as he turns back to me.

"It's kind of a post-game tradition," he explains. "We hit up the diner and gorge on those smiley cookies. You know the ones?"

"I do," I admit.

It's been years since I've had those particular treats, but even now, I can recall what it's like to sink my teeth into the thin sugar cookie coated in glazed icing.

Kara didn't mention that she had plans after the game, but I'll understand if she wants to go off with her teammates instead of hanging around with me, even though I haven't seen her in weeks.

I'm sure there's some sort of camaraderie-building or celebration needed, since they started the season with such a big win.

Maybe she'll bring me a few cookies afterward…

"I'm Penn Westbrook," he says easily, offering his hand for me to shake.

He smiles, and the hardness of his features is momentarily abated, so there's a sort of gentleness to the cut of his cheekbones.

The gesture has the audacity to make me feel all warm inside.

"Violet Smith," I answer.

I tentatively take his hand, and he takes control of the movement, locking his grasp around mine. His hands are rough, practically one big callus, and I kind of like the way it feels against my palms.

I stare at our joined hands for a second before I meet his gaze.

Once again, I'm awarded with a smile, only this one's smaller and somehow more personal.

It has the very dire side effect of drawing my gaze to the corner of his mouth.

"Who are you waiting—"

"Violet?" Kara's voice cuts across the lobby.

Her expression is pinched at first, taking in the sight of Penn and me, then amusement forms.

I drop his grasp and step back, moving to give my friend the fiercest hug I can offer.

"Where have you been?" I ask, squeezing her tight.

She laughs as we pull back, and I take in her freshly washed hair, which she's braided back off her face. There's also slight bruising on the bottom of her chin—one of many wounds she's likely sporting, a common side effect of playing such a rough game.

But I can tell from her radiant expression and easy demeanor that she's thrilled with how it went.

"Showering off," she answers, nodding to the door on the opposite side of the space. "The most contentious part of this whole deal. Did you know not all places have separate locker rooms for women and men? I hear that next week I have to get ready in a utility closet."

Even though I can still feel Penn's looming presence, I focus on Kara.

I'm here for *her* after all.

"You did great," I say honestly. "I have no idea how you saw that shot in the second period with all the traffic in front. It was awesome."

Kara merely shrugs. "There wasn't too much action for me in this one, but I'll take it."

"Seriously, you kicked ass," I say as I throw my arms around her shoulders once more. "I'm so proud of you."

Penn clears his throat. "You really did have an awesome game."

"You did, too," she says genuinely. "That one-handed shot almost went in."

"Your quick pass started it," Penn replies.

Kara laughs graciously, and as the sound peters off, we're left in somewhat stilted silence.

"Well, I should head out," Penn says finally.

"Okay," Kara returns. "See you later."

Penn readjusts his bag on his shoulder, and I don't miss how the muscles strain against his long-sleeved shirt.

"Violet," he says, offering my name as one word of finality.

"Penn," I return evenly.

He bites the edge of his lip before he retreats, and once he's through the double doors and firmly out of earshot, Kara's eyes widen.

Her smile turns devilish before she elbows me in what I think is delight. "What were you doing talking to Penn?"

"I was just waiting for you," I answer honestly.

She rolls her eyes. "Uh-huh."

I pause, assessing her. "Do you like him? Do you not like him? Isn't he the—"

"One who gave the statement to the school board in support of me joining the team?" Kara finishes for me. "Yes, that's him."

"That's what I thought."

"He's the captain."

I nod, even though I'm not sure what she's implying. "Okay."

"And he's probably the only player who is scouted more than me," she adds.

She's not bragging—she's simply trying to impress upon me what a big deal it was for him to speak up.

Penn went against his coaches and the boosters, who claimed her presence would be too much of a liability.

To say that Kara had a hell of a time getting her position is an understatement. It was all bureaucracy holding her back with a side of misogyny.

Of course, once her path was cleared, she made the team easily.

I loop my arm through hers. "Well, good for him."

"Yes," she agrees. "He's a good guy."

"But who cares about all that?" I deflect. "This night is about *you*."

She beams at me as we head out. "Thank you for being here for me."

"Are you joking? Nothing in this world would have kept me from witnessing your debut. Where else would I be if not supporting my best friend?"

She practically skips as we walk through the parking lot. "You are the best."

"I don't disagree with that," I say when we come to a stop in front of her car. "Don't you have plans tonight?"

Kara's brow furrows as she pops the trunk. "I thought we were hanging out."

"Well, yeah, I thought so, too," I say slowly. "But you said, 'See you later' to Penn, and I didn't know if you meant it or if it was just a casual dismissal or whatever. I mean, I totally understand if you want to go out with the team instead."

She shoves her bag inside, then presses the lift gate closed before she gives me a questioning glance. "The team?"

"Penn said it's tradition for everyone to go out to some diner after..." I trail off at the sight of her face falling.

She pulls her features into what I think is supposed to be an expression of indifference, but I don't buy it. I've seen enough false projections of emotion to know she's hurt to not have been included.

Physically, Kara is the toughest person I know, but mentally, she's really been through it these past few months.

I absolutely hate that she's gotten left out of something she fought so hard to be a part of. It makes me want to show up to that diner and throw those smiley cookies at her teammates.

Kara swallows audibly. "I didn't hear about that."

"Well, good," I say like it's no big deal. "Because we have a few hours until your curfew, and we have my debit card at our disposal. Do you want to get takeout from somewhere?"

She nods, but before we move, she reaches for my hand and squeezes it once.

That little motion says all the things she doesn't want to vocalize—and she doesn't need to—because I understand what she's feeling without her even saying a word.

FOUR

"What's up, Junebug?" Kara offers my sister a fist-bump as we walk into the kitchen.

June immediately brightens and returns the gesture. "I got a new game."

"Really?" Kara takes the chair beside her, settling into my usual spot. "How do you play?"

I tune out her explanation, already being familiar with the concept.

It's some sort of word challenge, and she's been obsessed with it ever since Ryan let her take over his old iPad. She's tried to get me to play it with her, but I'm as interested in it as she is in the nautical map app I have on my phone—which is to say, not remotely so.

I stretch my arms upward, trying to work out the tightness of my back muscles as I step toward the fridge.

Kara and I had an impromptu sleepover last night, which is relatively normal for us, but I somehow always manage to forget what a bed hog she is. And that she usually jars me awake at least twice in the middle of the night by catching me with an elbow as she tosses and turns.

"That's really cool," Kara says once June has finished babbling. "I can see why you like it so much."

June bounces with excitement in her chair. "And no one in the house has beaten my high score yet."

"You're a champ," Kara says on a laugh.

"I know it's after noon, but are you in the mood for pancakes?" I ask Kara.

"Definitely," June answers for her.

I shake my head, but I don't deny my sister's self-invitation. "Chocolate chip, then?"

June squeals as she pushes away her soggy cereal. "Yes, please!"

"Can you at least hit me with some blueberries?" Kara asks, patting her stomach. "Maybe some flax seeds if you have them?"

I know for a fact there's a six-pack underneath her hoodie, but I spare her my eyeroll.

She does like to indulge, appreciating my baking skills as much as everyone else, but she balances it out by also being conscious of eating healthy and supporting her physical activity.

Still, it's safe to say that last night's fast-food binge was out of the norm for her.

"I can do that," I agree.

"Thank you," Kara says before taking her turn with the game.

"June, if you clean up your cereal bowl, you can help me," I offer.

My sister's eyes go wide. "Really?"

I nod. "As long as we don't have a repeat of the omelet incident."

"I won't turn up the heat without asking you first," she promises as seriously as she can muster.

"Good."

The last time the two of us had the house to ourselves and cooked together, the smell of burnt eggs stayed in the kitchen for at least a week.

It's nice to have quiet time, but it happens so rarely. This weekend, however, my mom took Chloe to dance class, and Ryan, Kevin, and The Baby are off having "guy time," which usually involves some errands and maybe a treat.

Kara lets out a sigh as she sets down the iPad. "I can't beat you, June."

My sister lets out a laugh that's a little more maniacal than I would expect from her. "I told you."

I lean against the counter, double-checking that she isn't adding too much flour in her distraction, as Kara yawns and groans.

"How are you feeling today?" I ask her.

"Good." She stretches out her arms, then brings her hands up to examine them. "Well, my manicure's absolute trash, but other than that, I'm totally unscathed."

I quirk a brow, then nod toward her chin. "Totally?"

"Except for that," Kara amends.

"I can fix them," June says, handing the mixing bowl back to me. "Your nails, I mean."

I drop three blobs of batter onto the skillet. "How about after we eat?" I suggest. "Then I can redo yours, too, June."

She gives me a look like my words are too good to be true but doesn't question them. "Another sister spa party! Just like the last one."

I laugh at her enthusiasm, though a pang of guilt hits my chest at how easy it is to make her happy—and I wonder if my occasional brusqueness affects her just as much.

"Hell no," Kara cuts in.

June's nostrils flare. "What? Why not?"

"I'm not letting either of you near my hair."

I step forward to tug the end of Kara's perfectly ashy blonde hair. "I think we can leave this masterpiece to the true professionals."

"But Violet has all the measuring stuff and even a scale," June argues on my behalf. "Just like the hair people do on Instagram!"

"Just because your sister is a whiz at chemistry and numbers doesn't mean I should let her anywhere near this," Kara says as she fiddles with her braid.

"It's okay, June," I say as I flip the pancakes. "We can still do nails and maybe face masks later."

My sister ignores my words of reassurance. "Well, *Erica* said she might be game for adding some highlights to her hair..."

Kara tenses at the mention of her ex-friend, so I jump in.

"Well, Erica's on her six-month anniversary date all day today, so you'll have to settle for us."

Kara recovers, then forces her features into an exaggerated show of shock in June's direction. "Are you trying to manipulate me, Junebug?"

My sister lets out a very juvenile giggle. "No."

Kara jumps up, landing easily on two feet, then reaches out to tickle June's sides. "Are you sure about that?"

"Yes!" she insists while trying to hold in her chuckle.

"Admit it!" Kara yells as she doubles down on her effort.

"Never!"

"Do it!"

They both fall to the floor in a fit of laughter and playful banter, and I shake my head at their antics as I tend to our breakfast.

With the test batch perfectly browned, I begin another, adding blueberries to one and chocolate chips to the other, then wait patiently for the little bubbles to form so I can flip them.

I'm pleased that the texture and rise of the batter looks good, since it's been a while since I've tried to make pancakes and I went with my gut this time instead of carefully measuring the ingredients.

"I give. I give!" June's words are choppy since she's a little out of breath.

Kara releases her hold and lifts her hands in the air. "Victory!"

June huffs. "You don't have to go full sister spa day with us."

"And I'm still your favorite?" Kara asks, teeth bared with a wild smile.

June nods quickly. "Yes."

"Good." Kara offers her a hand, pulling them both back up.

"I thought I was your favorite, June?" I pout.

She holds up her hands defensively, waiting for me to attack her like Kara did. "You both are."

"I can accept that," I say as I fiddle with the spatula. "You want to flip these?"

"Yes," she says excitedly.

My phone buzzes, so as soon as my hands are free from tending to the stove, I slide my forearms on the smooth surface on the counter and hunch over as my screen unlocks.

The number isn't saved in my contacts, and I'm about to brush it off as one of those spam texts until I actually see the words.

And then I choke on my inhale.

"Who is it?" Kara asks as she leans over.

I tilt the phone so we can both read the message.

Hi Violet. It's your father. I'd like to speak with you soon. Let me know some days and times that you're available. Thanks.

I don't even know how to process what I'm seeing or how I'm feeling, but Kara scoffs at the phone.

"So, after months of not hearing from him, of him missing your birthday this year, of him not even caring about your senior year or your college applications, he just randomly decides to pop back in and send you that message out of the blue?"

I let out a sigh. "I guess?"

"Wow," she says while shaking her head. "Unbelievable. He's treating you like you're setting up a dentist appointment or something."

"It is kind of formal," I agree, chuckling lightly.

My dad and I don't really have the best relationship, but it's not from a lack of trying. When he is in town, he's present and doting and as attentive as he's supposed to be —it just hasn't happened in years.

He's a war correspondent, which means he's MIA for months at a time while on assignment in unsettled areas of the world and under constant threat of bombs and gunfire.

My mom made him stop telling me all the gruesome details of explosions he'd witnessed after they gave me nightmares at age twelve.

Even now that I'm eighteen and able to process the reality of his day to day, I don't enjoy picturing my biological father risking his life to chase down sources.

"Does he even know that you've applied to Cornell?" Kara asks.

It's a logical question, given it was a major source of nervousness and stress for months.

But the answer, of course, is no.

I shake my head in response, even though she probably already knows it.

Because that's not the only thing he hasn't been a part of—holidays, milestones, my perfect attendance award last year, my first school dance…the list goes on.

He loves his job, and I'm happy for him, but I'd be lying if I said I don't resent him just a little bit for everything he's missed.

I know I wasn't part of his grand life plan, but I wasn't part of Ryan's either, and he's been here for everything.

"How are you going to respond?" Kara asks, eyeing me. "If you're going to at all?"

I set down the phone and rub my eyes. "I don't know. I want to think about it, I guess. It's not like I owe him the courtesy of one."

"He's an ass," she says, then softens a bit. "I mean, I know he's your dad, but you don't have to feel obligated to talk to him."

"Yeah."

"You should do what *you* want." She pulls me in for a hug. "I'll be here for you regardless."

I'm grateful for the support and comfort. "Thank you."

"Just remember, you don't have to keep doing this to yourself," Kara adds.

"Doing this?" I question, stepping back.

"Act like it doesn't bother you."

"It doesn't," I say automatically.

She narrows her eyes with skepticism. "You can lie to yourself, but you can't lie to me."

I bite my bottom lip and consider her words. "It would be...nice...to talk to him. I guess? I don't know. After so many years of him disappearing and falling through on his promises, I've just been operating under the assumption that he doesn't exist, so it's a surprise when he does something to prove the opposite."

"Uh, Violet," June says, interrupting our conversation. "Are the pancakes supposed to look like this?"

I hurriedly cross over to the stovetop where June's been doing a good job of following the process.

"Oh yeah. These look great." I lay my excitement on thick to push away all the other feelings Kara's trying to force me to contend with. "Just the right amount of brown on the outside."

"Can we try them?" June asks while bouncing on her feet.

"Sure."

"I'll get the plates," Kara announces as she opens the cabinet.

We then make a big show of laying out our meal so it's photo-worthy, complete with placemats, full sets of silver, and glasses of juice.

After I've captured the perfect shot for my social accounts, Kara makes me take an impromptu photoshoot of her and June decorating the plates with whipped cream and more blueberries and chocolate.

By the time we actually dig into our breakfast, the pancakes are kind of cold, but we still eat them with enthusiasm in front of the television. June takes control of the remote, putting on some dramatic kids show that I only find partially annoying, and Kara wolfs down her entire plate before I even finish one of my pancakes.

After that, we move onto the nail-painting portion of the morning, and June's top coat has just finished drying by the time the garage door opens.

It's our last moment of peace before my other siblings storm the house, followed by my mom and Ryan, who both look relieved to be back home but exhausted by all the running around they've just done.

"Kara," my mom says in greeting as happiness overtakes the tired lines on her face.

"Hi, Jessica." Kara jumps up to give my mom a hug. "How are you?"

"Who cares about how we are?" Ryan asks, pulling her in for a hug next. "How are *you*? How was your big varsity debut?"

She laughs and bounces slightly on the balls of her feet. "It was pretty tame but good."

"She was awesome," I chime in.

"We'll have to wrangle everyone up and attend one of your games," Mom says.

"Can we paint our faces?" June asks.

"Yes!" Chloe mirrors. "I want a butterfly."

June rolls her eyes. "That's not what you do for a hockey game."

Chloe shrugs as she runs and jumps on the couch.

"Yeah, you fight!" Kevin declares while throwing punches in the air.

"Not quite," Kara tells him in an amused tone. "At least, I don't."

"Come on and help with these bags," Ryan says.

His words aren't directed to anyone in particular, but we all stand to help move the groceries toward the kitchen.

"I read the write-up of the game in the local paper," Ryan tells Kara as he heaves what I think is an entire bag of canned goods on the counter. "Seems you had an impressive save in the third period."

"I was in the paper?" she asks, eyes wide.

"Yeah." He crosses the kitchen and taps the article taped on the fridge. "I put it up this morning."

I didn't notice it there earlier.

And neither did Kara, apparently.

"Oh my gosh!"

She sprints over and gasps at her name and headshot, and I join her—at a much slower pace, of course.

Ryan put it in a place of prominence between the magnetized letters that The Baby frequently rearranges and a few drawings done by the twins years ago.

It warms my heart to see Kara's accomplishment forever captured in print and in our house.

Ryan winks at me, and it's not lost on me how special and thoughtful he is—and how lucky I am to have him in my life.

It's *almost* enough to make me forget about the text message from my biological father that may or may not get a response.

FIVE

"And then what happened?" Erica prompts.

"What do you mean?" I ask, watching her bat cookie crumbs from her lips.

"The game just ended?"

"Oh," I say. "Uh, yeah."

She lets out a sigh like I'm holding something back.

It's just the two of us in broadcast class today because Aksa and Emily are on a field trip to a museum with their art class.

I've given her all the information about the game and then some because she's asked dozens of questions. And honestly, I'm not sure what Erica is trying to get from this play-by-play of Friday's game.

"No last-minute shots or trick plays?"

I shake my head. "Nope."

"Well, did—"

"Erica," I cut in, letting my exasperation show. "Do you want me to find a stream of the game so you can watch it yourself? I feel like I've spent a lot of time answering your questions, and I don't know what else to say."

"Sorry for being *interested* in the game," she says defensively. "You know how much I enjoy hockey."

I tilt my head, assessing her. "Is that even true?"

"What? Of course," she sputters. "I'm dating Alex, after all."

I purse my lips.

I suppose that's enough justification for her sudden interest in a rival team—after all, Alex and Kara's teams are slated to play each other in just a few weeks. But until she started dating Alex, she was adamant that all sports were a big waste of time.

"Right," I say, letting it roll off. "I just don't have any other explanation or details for you. Sometimes I barely feel like I'm keeping up with how fast everything moves."

"Okay," she relents.

I take that as a sign that I can finally turn my attention back to my assignment.

But no matter how much I mentally will her to do the same with whatever homework she's ignoring at the moment, I can *sense* the wheels in her mind moving about everything other than school.

Plus, she keeps clicking the end of her pen as she fidgets, and the sound of it repeats enough to grate and distract me.

I read the definition of oxidation reduction multiple times before I give up, grinding my teeth as I glance at her again.

"What is it, Erica?"

She gives me a small smile. "Well, it's just that Alex

was saying those hockey boys over at that school are, like, *rough*."

"Isn't that true for all hockey players?" I argue. "I mean, you are dating one. So maybe you should really watch out."

I'm trying to tease, but my annoyance comes through enough that it seems like I'm snapping at her.

Erica seems unfazed, though. "Yes, exactly. That's why Alex knows so much. Apparently, he played them in the playoffs last year, and they were brutal. Dirty shots. And a fight that got one of their players ejected."

"I didn't see anything like that on Friday," I say dismissively.

In fact, aside from the increased size of the players and my anger at the team for not including Kara in their post-game outing, it was pretty much just like any of her other games over the last several years.

I'd never say that to Kara, of course, because the circumstances were very special.

"Well, just look out for yourself," Erica says.

My brows furrow as I glance at her, wondering where this is coming from.

Surely there's no way she could know about Penn's lingering and our introduction…

"I mean, if you're going to be spending time there with Kara, I don't want you to get dragged into something you're not comfortable with," Erica presses. "She can take care of herself, obviously."

"I'm not sure what you're implying," I say honestly. "Do you think I'm going to have a total personality snap and jump onto the ice and start punching people in the face or something?"

She waves me off. "Just what I said."

Part of me wants to use the hall pass I got from Aksa to escape this questioning, but I think it would turn into a whole thing.

"Can we not talk about this anymore?" I ask instead. "This is taking up far too much of my mental capacity for the day."

She rolls her eyes. "Fine, fine. Whatever. I've been meaning to talk to you about the bake sale, anyway."

"What bake sale?" I ask tentatively.

"All the clubs around school are doing fundraisers during the week of Thanksgiving," she explains. "You know, to help fund all the programs and keep them going."

"But this isn't really a club," I protest, glancing around our makeshift newsroom.

It's not exactly glamorous, but it's functional.

We're sitting in one of the many clusters of desks, like a normal classroom, but the space is split in half with a glass wall. Behind it, there's a camera, a few monitors, and a table in front of a green screen.

"I mean, yeah, we have to stay after school sometimes," I continue. "But we're also getting graded for our work. And we have those current event pop quizzes."

"I'm talking about improv club," Erica says with exasperation.

I meet her gaze. "You mean the one I'm not part of?"

"Well, I was hoping you wouldn't mind donating something..." She trails off, having the decency to look a little bit sheepish. "Maybe your caramel pumpkin pie? And more of these cookies for sure. Oh, and those cinnamon brownies you made! The almond flour is surprisingly good."

I fix my gaze out the window, needing a moment to push down my irritation, which is surfacing too easily today.

Or lately, I guess.

I can't pinpoint the source of it, but Erica definitely isn't helping.

It might be a culmination of things—Kara's exclusion last Friday, the text from my biological dad I can't bring myself to respond to, the chaos at home, or the fact that I've somehow become Erica's personal culinary arts professional, expected to produce treats at her beck and call.

Maybe it's my fault for being so excited about finding something I loved and sharing it, not realizing it would create expectations and demands other than my enjoyment.

Baking started out as a fun hobby for me because it turned chemistry experiments into real, edible results, as opposed to using chemicals that could cause burns and other health hazards.

I love spending my weekends inventing new recipes or tweaking existing ones—like seeing how only using the whites instead of entire eggs can change the texture of muffins.

It's a fun activity for me, especially in the colder months because I can't spend as much time outside. I'm not an outdoorsy person, but my love for science manifests in many forms. I could spend an afternoon lying on a blanket, watching the clouds go by, and noting their different patterns.

Today isn't a good day for that, though, because the sky is clear and a crisp shade of blue.

I should appreciate one of the final sunny days of fall,

but I'm actually a little bothered by the stream of light coming in through the window. I know, logically, it means that the cooler temperatures are holding less moisture in the air, but I find comfort in the little fluffy blobs in the sky.

It definitely beats being in school or getting guilted into favors for my friends.

"So, what do you say? Will you help me out? Please?"

Erica tucks her hair behind her ears as she eyes me.

It's a gesture I've seen hundreds of times over the years, and it means she really wants something but is uncertain about the outcome.

But I know I will likely spend my free time baking anyway, and if it helps her and her club, I guess I don't mind.

"Sure," I say.

She instantly brightens. "Great! So, I'll need everything the Tuesday before Thanksgiving, obviously, so we can have time to actually sell them before the holiday. Do you need me to do anything for you?"

I shake my head. "I think I've got it under control. I'll let you know what I come up with."

"You're not going to follow my suggestions?" Erica asks, taken aback, then catches herself. "Right, of course. Whatever you think will be good will work."

"Yeah," I say flatly.

She nods at me before finally turning her attention back to her homework.

Of course, now I'm totally distracted, thinking through all the possibilities. Instead of focusing on my assignment, I pull out my phone and flip to the app where I store all my recipes, along with photos and corresponding notes.

They're meticulously organized by type—cookies, cakes, muffins, etc.—but nothing jumps out at me.

Erica's suggestions were fine, but I'm wondering if I should try something else. I swipe my finger over to the browser and am searching for fall-themed baked goods when my phone vibrates with an incoming message.

Not many people text me in general, let alone during school hours.

My stomach sinks in the five seconds it takes me to move between apps because I'm worried it's going to be my father, following up on his previous message.

Thankfully, it's just Kara.

Viiiiiii.

I smile as my thumbs type *Kaaaaa* then hit send.

She replies with the eyeroll emoji, then another message right after it. *Sooooo.*

So, what?

The guys on the team are having a party on Saturday.

She doesn't immediately start typing, providing me with additional details, and I'm worried that she heard about it through the grapevine and didn't score an invitation herself.

Oh? I prompt.

Yeah! Penn actually came by at lunch and personally apologized that I didn't get included on Friday.

That's good.

He thought one of the defenders had invited me to the diner, so he didn't...but yeah, now I'm on the team GROUP TEXT and everything!!!!

I smirk, but I'm ridiculously happy for her. *They grow up so fast…*

Shut it.

I let out a laugh, loving that she is probably doing the same on the other end.

Erica huffs. "Who are you texting?"

"Kara," I answer, keeping my eyes fixed on the screen.

Another message comes through. *Will you please please pleaseee go with me?*

What? I balk before I type again. *Why?*

Because I don't really know any of these guys yet, and I don't want to be the person who stands awkwardly in the corner of the room all night.

"What does she want?" Erica asks, feigning nonchalance.

"Me to go to a party with her this weekend," I answer automatically.

But isn't it like a team bonding thing? I clarify. *Wouldn't it be weird if I went?*

Penn said it's an open invite, and I could bring whoever I wanted. Apparently, a lot of the guys bring their significant others or whatever.

I get a rush of jittery nerves at the thought of seeing him again, which is absolutely ridiculous.

Clinically speaking, I think my body reacts—then and now—to being attracted to him, sending out waves of dopamine, norepinephrine, and adrenaline.

But I'm not vain enough to think that he felt the same way or that's why Kara suddenly got included with encouragement to bring along anyone she wanted.

"A party?" Erica says.

"Uh-huh." I tap my fingers on the top of the desk, mind still occupied by thoughts of Penn. "Her, and the team, and other people from her school, I guess."

"Violet!" Erica's sharp tone, along with the wave of her hand, captures my full attention. "Did I not just warn you about her teammates? If they behave like that in front of referees, parents, and a rink full of spectators, who knows how they'll act at a party?"

I blink as I take in her forcefulness.

Erica's always been headstrong, but this sense of underlying panic seems misplaced, and I don't buy that she's being genuine.

"What's this really about?" I ask.

"Wh-what?" Erica sputters. "What do you mean?"

"Erica," I say slowly. "Are you really afraid for my life because I'm going to a party with people from another school?"

The words sit between us for a beat before she answers.

"I just…" She pauses and takes a breath. "I don't know. It's just, like, you and I haven't really hung out much."

I try to keep my expression neutral. "I see you every single day at school."

"Obviously. But not outside of that."

Ever since Erica and Kara had their falling out—or fight or whatever the hell happened between them—I've picked up on some jealousy on Erica's part.

She treats people like chess pieces, calculating how they move and fit into her life, and I haven't really noticed I'm one of them until now.

I'm her homework guru. Alex is her constant source of entertainment and pride. Emily is who she talks to when she needs to be fawned over. And she sees Aksa as her rival in a way.

Still, though, we've been best friends forever, and I'm hopeful outside of school we can rediscover common ground that's not calculus.

"Okay," I say easily. "Let's do something on Friday."

"Yes," she says brightly, then falters. "Oh, wait. I have plans with Alex to go to the movies. Maybe you could join us?"

"Hard pass," I answer, then quickly add, "No offense. I don't feel like third-wheeling on date night."

I made that mistake once early on in their relationship.

It was the most uncomfortable dinner of my life, sitting opposite them in a booth while they fed each other and kissed and whispered.

"What about Sunday?" I suggest. "We could do something in the afternoon, like go to that—"

"Can't," she cuts in. "Alex and I are going to visit his grandmother in Erie for the day."

"Okay then." I shrug. "Maybe some other time."

She frowns, and I hope she's piecing together that this situation is of her own making.

"Well, we'll figure out something soon," Erica says.

"Of course."

I don't think we will, though, and I find that I'm actually just fine with it, especially as I refocus on my phone and send a text to Kara.

I'm in.

SIX

"Violet?"

My mom taps on my closed door with her knuckles, but she enters my room before I can answer.

We've had multiple conversations attempting to establish boundaries in our crowded house—like knocking before entering. She's got the first part down, which I appreciate, but she seems to always forget to wait for my verbal permission.

It's frustrating how accustomed I have become to the lack of privacy.

I can't even get twenty minutes alone to get ready without Chloe busting in and peppering me with questions or June trying to pilfer something from my closet.

Or my mom perching on the edge of the bed and watching me do the final roll of my curling iron.

"You look fantastic," she gushes.

"Thanks," I say as I pull the wand out of my hair.

"Is that a new style?"

I nod and flip the off switch. "I'm trying for loose waves, and I think I nailed it."

"Definitely," she says. "And your makeup! It looks great. Your outfit, too."

I quirk a brow at her excessive complimenting. "Thank you."

She glances around the room like it's the first time she's ever been in here, taking care to admire the little plastic star decorations that Kara helped me put on the ceiling.

I turn back to the mirror and appraise my appearance, wondering if my mom was laying the praise so thick for a reason.

My normally straight and slightly frizzy hair is now styled, and I've taken care to put on dark eye makeup with winged eyeliner. This look generally makes me look more mature than I do with a fresh face, but I don't think I've overdone it.

My clothing is the same as it usually is—high-waisted jeans with a white cut-off shirt—only I've dressed it up with some dangly earrings and a necklace.

"So." My mom clears her throat. "Your first big senior year party…"

In the reflection, I see her purse her lips and drop her gaze to the carpet.

And then I notice her splotchy cheeks.

"Are you *crying*?" I ask, appalled.

She looks at me head-on and in time for one single tear to roll down her cheek. "Just a little bit."

I groan. "Mom…"

She laughs before she bats it away, and I soften and move to sit beside her. She wraps her arms around me and drops her head on my shoulder as soon as I sink into the mattress.

"It's just a party," I remind her, patting her hand.

"I know. But it has me thinking about how far away you're going to be next year."

"We don't even know if Cornell is a done deal yet," I say in reassurance. "And a six-hour drive isn't the worst."

She drops our embrace so she can look me in the eye. "I already feel like I miss you."

"I am right here."

"I know. And I know it sounds silly, but it's true." She reaches over and squeezes my hand. "You promise if you need anything, you'll call me? No matter what time of night or what situation you're in?"

I smirk. "Tonight or when I'm at college?"

"Anytime for the rest of your life," she says seriously.

"I'll be fine, Mom." I try to withhold the whine from my tone, but it's definitely there. "Really."

She smiles slowly, but eventually it forms into a full grin. "Yes. You will."

The doorbell rings, indicating Kara's arrival, and I let out a relieved breath.

My mom waves a hand. "Go on with your night and enjoy getting away from your overbearing mother."

"You're not overbearing," I tell her.

She gives me a questioning look. "You don't think so?"

"A little clingy and unaware of boundaries," I tease. "But it's annoying. Not stifling."

That makes her laugh. "Fair point. Just...do me a favor and try not to get into too much trouble tonight, okay?"

I stand, but before I leave the room, I give her one final

look. "Out of curiosity, what do you think is an adequate amount of trouble for me to get into?"

"Just go," she says, fighting off her laugh.

I happily oblige, breezing past my siblings and Ryan—who all chat up Kara near the front door—then she and I skip to her car.

And, finally, we're off, speeding into the night with the windows cracked and the music blaring.

It feels like freedom.

But I do have some underlying nerves.

I don't really know what to expect with the party in general, but I also don't know if I'm being ridiculous for letting myself be excited about seeing Penn again. I kind of hate that I've thought about him so many times since our brief introduction because I don't know if I'm just letting my brain latch onto the possibility of him.

But, I suppose, I'll find out soon enough.

I think Kara is also jittery, but she's trying to hide it as she sings along to some new pop punk track, pretending her incessant tapping on the steering wheel is due to the rhythm instead of anxiety.

When we park on the street and walk up to the house, I'm a little bit more at ease because of how normal this feels. The neighborhood is well within her school district, but it has similar vibes to mine—a quiet street and plenty of space between houses to have yards but not so much that trick-or-treating would be a nightmare.

I do, however, think it's an odd choice to prop the front door open with a fancy dining room chair.

But as I cross the threshold, I immediately understand that the chilly night air is a reprieve for all the partygoers—

who create a heatwave in the living room with all their dancing and general enjoyment of the festivities.

"What do you want to do?" I ask Kara over the music.

"Let's go over there," she suggests, nodding toward the dining room. "I think I'll feel less awkward with a drink."

I nod as she reaches for my hand, then we make our way through the crowd of people, some of whom I vaguely recognize as her teammates.

I'm helpless to do anything other than let her lead me, so I keep my gaze focused on how relaxed and cool she looks in her high-top Nikes, shredded jeans, and oversized t-shirt.

We eventually make it to the dining room where there's a table full of haphazardly arranged bottles and a nearby antique credenza covered in unopened cans.

I give her hand a reassuring squeeze before we shift our attention to our options. They're pretty limited, and Kara and I are both out of our element—aside from a few sips of wine on special occasions, neither of us have drank alcohol.

"This looks a little intimidating," I murmur, unsure of where to even start.

She nods and reaches for a can of Sprite and two empty cups. "Maybe we'll go for this until we get the lay of the land?"

"Sounds good to me."

I accept a cup once she's filled both. "Cheers to us."

"Wow," Kara says after a sip. "This is strong."

I laugh and play along. "So…alcohol-y."

"Pretty much a regular bartender over here." She flips her hair over her shoulder. "I only accept cash tips. Of course, *you* get the best friend discount."

Our banter is interrupted by a loud round of cheering on the other side of the room where there's a game of beer pong in progress. I've never played myself, but I've learned enough from movies to understand it appears someone has landed a ball in the remaining cup, claiming victory.

And, of course, my gaze immediately lands on Penn.

He's smiling widely as his teammates whoop and pat him on the back, and they seem just as thrilled that he's scored the winning shot as if they were on the ice.

Penn holds up his hands, trying to quell the chaos around him, but he can't stop laughing enough to tell them to stop as they exaggeratedly fawn over him.

He throws his head back as his mirth ratchets up, and when he brings his chin down again, his eyes meet mine.

I swallow a mouthful of Sprite and pretend like his recognition of my presence doesn't jolt my entire being.

It's funny how our bodies can react to these little moments, building up anticipation and excitement.

And that's just from one shared look.

Turning back to Kara, I can only hope she doesn't comment on how flushed my cheeks suddenly are.

"God, the testosterone in here is stifling," Kara says with a sigh, eyeing her teammates as they finally settle down.

I clear my throat. "I thought you'd be used to it by now. Since you're one of them and everything."

She takes another drink. "I've been on the team for, like, two seconds."

"That's not true, you've had three games and multiple prac—"

"Hey, Kara," Penn cuts in as he approaches. "I'm glad you could make it."

"Penn," she returns.

They clink plastic cups, and I hold still, not wanting to disrupt any potential bonding.

But Penn turns to me directly, giving me no choice other than to will my heart to stop pounding in my chest as he offers me a wry smile.

"Hey, Violet."

I can't tell if the intonation of my name is different from the way he says Kara's—and that thought alone makes me worry that I'm reading too much into things.

Kara's attention flicks between us, then she takes a sip to hide her curious gaze.

"Thanks for having us," I say cordially. "How are you?"

He bows his head, almost mocking my formality. "Good. And you?"

"Good," I answer.

"Well, that's…good," Penn says jovially. "I wouldn't want anyone to have a bad time in my house."

I suddenly have a renewed urge to take in the space. "You live here?"

"Only since I was born. It's got everything a person needs. A kitchen, multiple bathrooms, a spacious backyard—"

"And a divine liquor selection," a booming voice adds, worming into our conversation.

I turn toward the voice and find the massive, red-haired guy from the lobby.

Even though he's in a casual shirt and jeans tonight instead of a bulky sweatshirt, I'm still impressed by the sheer size of him. On his own, he looks slightly out of place, but as I take him in beside Kara and Penn, along with the other athletes in the background, *I'm* the one who feels like I don't belong.

"Charlie," Kara says in greeting.

I can't tell if it's animosity or respect I'm picking up in her tone.

"Well, if it isn't the starting goalie who took my job," Charlie says sourly before downing half of his drink.

Kara laughs confidently and crosses her arms over her chest. "That's me."

My eyes bug out slightly, and I hold my breath while I wait for some sort of verbal sparring to ensue.

But Charlie only laughs and pulls her in for a hug.

I let out a sigh of relief, which doesn't go unnoticed by Penn.

"You want to be my partner next round?" Charlie asks Kara.

"Maybe," she answers nonchalantly before turning to Penn. "Is he good? Or did you have to carry the team?"

"Oh, I totally carried the team," Penn says with a laugh.

Charlie holds his hand to his chest, acting affronted. "Hey now."

"I love you, buddy." Penn pats him on the back. "But I don't think there is anything in this world you could bribe me with to have you as my partner again."

"Wow," Charlie says, shaking his head.

Penn gives an exaggerated wince. "Sorry."

"And to think I call you my best friend," the redhead mutters.

"What else is there to do around here?" Kara asks. "Are beer pong and dancing our only options?"

"Well, there's cornhole in the backyard," Penn suggests, leaning over to peek out the window.

"And flip cup in the kitchen," Charlie adds.

Kara wrinkles her nose as she fiddles with the lip of her drink.

"No, no, no," Charlie chides, putting a massive arm around her shoulders.

"What?" Kara balks.

"I can't have you attend your first team party with that attitude," he tells her. "We're supposed to be celebrating this season and enjoying our youth."

"Yeah," Penn echoes.

Kara tilts her head to the side as she appraises them both. "Well, what else have you got, then?"

"I do love a good jigsaw puzzle," I finally speak up, glancing at the stack of boxes in the corner.

"And those magazines from the early 2000s look tempting," Kara says. "It's an impressive collection."

"Absolutely not," Charlie insists.

Penn frowns at the three of us, then gets a gleam in his eye as his lips turn upward. "I've got *Mario Kart*."

"Yes!" Charlie says eagerly. "We're doing it."

Before either Kara or I can agree, he swipes a bottle from the table and practically pushes us up the stairs.

And then everything gets a little blurry.

SEVEN

Vodka is absolutely atrocious.

I barely manage to choke it down, learning it's called a *shot* for a reason—as opposed to a *sip*.

I promptly cut myself off, assuming that no amount of positive effects could be worth that, but I'm the only one. Penn, Charlie, and Kara take another, then they each make a mixed drink while they chatter on.

I'm already feeling the effects of those few measly ounces, almost embarrassingly so, but I try to act casual and hold myself normally as I look around Penn's bedroom.

His *bedroom*.

Where he gets ready in the morning, picks out his clothes, spends his time, and sleeps.

And I'm in it now, sitting on the gray carpet.

His matching set of bedroom furniture is oddly endearing, even though it's just a common dark wood.

Sometimes I look at things and imagine the exact moment someone decided to purchase it. Like, did he go with his parents to the furniture store, then walk up and down the long aisles of staged rooms to land on this one? Or did his parents pick it out for him after some sales associate pitched them the details of the quality and longevity of the pieces?

That answer might give me a little more insight into Penn's life, but in no way am I going to ask such a weird question after being in here mere minutes, so I look for other clues.

There are little signs of his life as a hockey player on top of his dresser—a few trophies and some gear—but nothing more that indicates anything about him other than the sport that takes up so much of his attention.

At some point in time, I think, there were pictures or posters on the walls. I can just make out a few dots that are clearly old tack marks, illuminated by the Christmas lights that have been nailed above them.

But the most defining part of the room is the massive television and collection of gaming consoles beneath it.

"Is that an original Wii?" I ask, squinting at the white console.

I've interrupted their conversation about next week's game, and even though no one looks like they mind, I feel momentarily bad about it.

Penn scoots toward me, then leans his back against the footboard of his bed so he faces the unit. "It is. And that's the original PlayStation right next to it. I've also got the original Xbox, a Sega Genesis, a GameCube, and—"

"No way," Kara jumps in. "Is that a Nintendo64?"

"Yeah," Penn says enthusiastically. "Your favorite?"

She brightens. "Absolutely."

"Games are in that drawer." He points with his sock-clad foot. "If you want to pick one for us?"

But before Kara can move to rifle through the selection, Charlie puts a hand on her arm.

"If I'm going to beat your ass at a video game, it has to be something designed after we were born," he says.

"Well, I'm not playing any of those shooter games. I was promised Mario." Kara grins devilishly. "But no one specified which version."

"Well done." Penn nods approvingly. "How about we play on the Switch, though, since the graphics are better?"

Kara merely raises a challenging brow at Charlie. "You in?"

"Another shot first," he says.

"Deal," she agrees.

Penn busies himself with changing over the plugs while his teammates argue over the size of the pours, and he hands me a controller as they wince at the taste.

"Thanks," I say, gripping the smooth plastic in my hands.

"Do you know how to play?" Penn asks.

"Kara's cousin has an N64," I tell him. "He let us play for a bit last summer over Fourth of July weekend."

Kara snorts. "If by 'let us play,' you mean I threatened him until he handed it over."

"I'm sure he was *really* scared," Charlie says sarcastically.

"He was," she retorts, holding up a fist.

"Okay, okay, enough," Penn says as he gets the game cued up. "The controls are pretty similar to what you're used to, but they're just in different spots."

It's a little awkward to hold the small remote as opposed to the two-handed controller I'm familiar with, but at least I'm able to get comfortable with where all the buttons are while he picks the number of players and the length and type of race.

Finally, it's our turn to select our characters.

"I call Yoshi," Penn announces.

"No!" Kara howls. "He's mine."

I laugh. "Kara and I had to take turns last time we played."

"We can all be Yoshi," Penn explains. "The game developers in their infinite wisdom foresaw his popularity, so we can all be different colors if we want."

"Really?" I gleefully select his cute little dinosaur face. "I'm getting him, too, then."

"We can't all be Yoshi," Charlie protests in an exasperated tone.

"Why not?" I ask, flipping through all the available options. "There are more than enough colors."

"To be anything other than the original green Yoshi is a crime against humanity," he says ominously.

"Oh, is it?" Kara makes a big show of selecting the yellow one for herself.

Charlie merely groans in response.

"Come on, you take the red one," she encourages him.

"Are we all matching our hair color?" Penn teases.

"Yes," I say immediately as I pick the orange Yoshi.

"But there's no brown," Kara says. "So whatever you pick, Penn, Violet gets to dye your hair that color."

"Really?" he asks, eyeing me.

"Definitely," I say, finding some confidence—thanks to Kara's words and the slight buzz of alcohol in my veins.

Penn smirks at me, then makes his choice.

"Blue?" Charlie scoffs. "I was hoping you'd go with one of our team colors."

"It's the closest thing to violet," Penn explains. "They've shorted us by not having a purple Yoshi."

I bark out a laugh, but I'm at a loss for what to say.

"Perfect," Kara declares. "Vi, you already have all the right stuff from doing June's hair."

"Who's June?" Penn asks.

"My sister," I tell him. "Well, one of them. I have two sisters and two brothers, but they—"

"Are we playing or what?" Charlie cuts in.

"Let them talk," Kara snaps at him. "You're so impatient. That's your problem."

"My *problem*?" Charlie repeats.

"Yeah. I never thought I'd meet a goalie who is *too quick* to move, but you have to find a balance between impulsiveness and the correct reaction."

Charlie shakes his head. "Are we talking video games or hockey here?"

"Let's just play," I say quickly.

"We have to choose our vehicles first," Penn advises, turning back to the screen.

I flip through the available bodies, wheels, and umbrellas and choose a cool-looking skeleton motorcycle.

Unsurprisingly, Kara selects the same, and then we're all dropped on the starting line.

"This is my favorite," Penn says. "Sweet Sweet Canyon."

I blink at the quick overview of the course. "It's...pastry themed?"

"Look at the little gingerbread men cheering us on," he says cheerfully. "And the tunnel is just one giant donut."

"You a big fan of dessert?" Kara asks.

Penn nods. "Best and most important meal of the day."

She lets out a ridiculous laugh. "Oh, this is too good."

"Why's that?" Penn asks, brows pinched together.

"It's time," I say, trying to pull their attention to the game.

But I don't miss the pointed look Kara sends my direction.

As the countdown begins, Kara elbows Charlie. "I hope you're a better driver than a goalie."

"Yeah, yeah," he says as we start.

The three of them spend the first lap laughing and trying to race through their slightly impaired motor skills, but I hunker down, determined to overcome the unfamiliarity of the track and the buttons.

In the second lap, the competition increases. There's less playful ribbing and more sounds of frustration and yelling at the screen as Kara pulls into first place. She drops a bunch of bananas behind her in an attempt to slow us down, and I drive straight into one, spinning out and giving Penn room to move into second place.

Special music sounds as we begin the third and final loop around the brightly lit and slightly treacherous track, and despite its cuteness, it's intense. I miss the blocks to get any little bonus items, but Charlie somehow randomly gets a rocket boost then a shell. He sends the latter hurling toward Kara, who yells as she's knocked off the course.

"Noooooooo!" Kara whines.

"LET'S GO!" Charlie screams as he earns first place. "LET'S GO, BABY!"

He jumps up and does a cringe-worthy but fantastic victory dance, swirling his hips as his hands pump in the air.

"Excessive celebration, much?" Kara says with a huff.

"Someone's a sore loser," Charlie says as he settles back down, unable to stop grinning from ear to ear.

"She definitely is," I agree.

Penn shakes his head. "I can't see it."

I smile at him. "One time, my younger brother beat her in checkers, and she locked herself in my room for an hour to cool down."

He laughs. "Really?"

"And I should explain that he's *four*," I add.

"Wow," he breathes. "I'll keep that in mind."

"All right, enough poking fun at my expense," Kara says. "Now, come on, let's do best of three."

"You're on," Charlie says, renewing his gaze.

Penn winks at me as the countdown begins again.

By the time we resurface from several more rounds of competition, I have to stretch my fingers from the intensity of my grip.

Charlie has won twice, Penn three times, and me once, which means Kara has nothing to show for all her smack talk.

"I quit," she announces, setting aside her controller.

"Here," Penn says, offering her the bottle. "For soul soothing."

She laughs as she waves him off. "I appreciate that, but

I think food is what's needed at this point. I want to soak up some of this alcohol and also eat my feelings."

"I can get down with that," Charlie says as he stands and stretches.

"There might be some pizza left in the kitchen," Penn offers.

Charlie holds out a hand for Kara, but she glares at him.

"I've got it." She bats his hand away and jumps up easily. "Let's go."

It's not that I'm not hungry—because I could probably wolf down one thousand slices of cheesy goodness right about now—but I catch Penn's easy posture and smile, and I don't move a muscle.

He doesn't either, and I'm not sure what this means.

But I'm going to roll with it.

When neither of us rises, Kara takes the hint. "We'll do a recon mission and come back with what we find," she announces. "You good with that, Violet?"

I nod. "I am."

She smiles and passes through the doorway, tripping and teasing Charlie all the way down the hall and threatening him with payback for winning so many games.

I turn to Penn with the intention of asking if he wants to play again, but he speaks first.

"So, you have two sisters and two brothers?"

"Oh," I say, surprised by his question. "Yes. June is my younger sister—"

"Who has purple hair that will soon match mine," Penn reminds me.

"Right." I let out a chuckle, unable to decipher how serious he is. "Uh, and then there are the twins, Chloe and

Kevin, and my youngest brother, Brandon, who everyone just calls 'The Baby.'"

"Who beat Kara in checkers?" Penn asks. "Kevin or The Baby?"

"The Baby."

"Wow."

I laugh as the memory surfaces. "What's even worse is he was clinging to his little stuffed Yoda while he dealt the final blow."

"Well, he had the power of the Force on his side, so I can understand how he would've defeated a mere mortal like Kara."

I snort. "You should tell her that. It would definitely make her feel better about losing."

"Maybe I will," he says as he pushes his hair away from his eyes. "That's a lot of siblings, though."

"I guess it is. Are you an only child?" I help myself to another drink, watching as a flash of *something* hits his features.

"Yeah," he says quickly. "Do you have your own bedrooms?"

I find the question odd, but I still answer it. "I do, but my other siblings share."

"What color is your room?" Penn asks next. "What does it look like?"

"White walls and furniture," I reply as I brush my hands on the carpet. "But I have a blue rug."

"What shade of blue? Are we talking the sky or something more—"

"Do you want to be an FBI agent or some sort of interrogator in the future?" I turn slightly so we're facing each other instead of sitting side by side.

He quirks a brow. "No. Why?"

"Have you ever watched one of those fictional crime-solving shows?" I ask him. "Like where they dramatize uncovering the killer's motive and solving the case?"

"No."

"It seems like you're trying to build a profile of a murder suspect."

Penn laughs and shakes his head. "What?"

"You're asking a lot of questions."

"Well, I'm trying to get to know you. You know, people do that by making conversation."

"Then let me ask a question," I counter. "It doesn't need to be a one-sided conversation."

"Okay," Penn allows. "It's your turn, then."

He makes a show of pressing his lips in a thin line, and I spend a beat too long wishing he wouldn't hide his perfect cupid's bow.

"What do you want to do when you graduate?" I ask. "You're a senior, too, right?"

"Yeah. I've got a few scholarship offers."

"I know. Kara told me. Said you're the only player who got more offers than her."

"She *is* competitive," Penn says with a smile.

"Where are your offers to? Unless you're not allowed to share?"

"No, it's fine. Some school in California I've never heard of. One in Canada, and one in the upper part of Minnesota that might as well be Canada. Two in Michigan. But I think I'm leaning toward Colgate."

I recognize the name, of course, because it's the same school Kara is planning to attend next year.

And because of that, I know it's only an hour and a half away from Cornell, my number one choice.

"And, uh," I stammer, searching for another question. "What are you going to major in?"

He rubs his knuckles on his cheek, and I realize that, for the first time in my presence, he's a little embarrassed.

"I haven't thought that far ahead, honestly," he hedges. "The past year has just been about studying and training and playing, and I'm just focusing on having an awesome season."

"That's good," I tell him.

I find his genuine uncertainty and ambiguity to be surprisingly refreshing—and validating as I wait for my future to be decided.

"Is it?" Penn poses as his gaze cuts into mine. "I'm not sure my guidance counselor agrees. What are *you* planning on studying? That is, if I can ask a question again now..."

I bite back the smile. "Well, the technical name of my major depends on where I get in, but I think I want to be a meteorologist."

"Really?" Penn says, eyes widening in delight. "I've never met anyone who *wanted* to do that."

I shrug. "Now you have."

"Do you want to be on the news? Like, reporting the weather every day at six o'clock?"

"Oh, absolutely not," I say quickly. "I'm actually in a broadcast journalism class at school, and that very thing is my worst nightmare. Being on camera at the center of attention is definitely not for me."

"Says the person with bright orange hair," Penn retorts.

I twirl the ends self-consciously. "I just thought it looked cool."

"I do, too," he says softly.

"But yeah," I continue, pressing the topic forward. "I really like science, and while there's a few different ways I can spin it, I think I want to do something hands-on. But with data instead of chemicals, if that makes sense. Like, I could study the atmosphere or climate change or something. I don't know. The programs sounded interesting, so I went for it."

"So, you could say you're a little *up in the air* right now?" Penn teases.

I laugh. "Maybe my future is. And I guess we all are. In some ways, we're helpless against the weather. Like, we pour all this money into disaster recovery and oceanic studies and exploring space, but every single time it rains, we run around with flimsy little umbrellas and hope our windshield wipers will help."

Penn tilts his head. "You know, I've never thought about it like that."

"I think about it all the time," I admit.

I pull my phone from my pocket, then slide my thumb across the screen and show him the folder I've dedicated solely to weather, ocean, and sky monitoring apps.

He leans closer to look. "I didn't even know there were so many options. I just use the one that came with my phone."

"Oh, yeah, there are tons. The best ones aren't free, of course, but—"

With the quickness only an athlete can pull off, Penn

snatches the device out of my hand.

"Wait, what are you doing?" I demand.

"Just adding my number," he says nonchalantly.

"Why?"

His fingers move so quickly that he has already saved his information. "Why what?"

"Why did you give me your number?" I clarify as he hands my phone back and I lock the screen.

"I was hoping we could do this again sometime," Penn says easily. "But instead of a party where we hide out in my bedroom, maybe we could go get food or something."

I blink. "Why do you want to do that?"

"Why do I—" Penn stops himself and smiles. "I'm trying to ask you out. Like on a date. Because I like you."

"I understand what the implication is," I say honestly. "And I'm not being shy or modest. I just want to under-stand why. Since the moment we met, you've had this, like, intensity."

Penn laughs, fully unencumbered. "You think *I* am intense?"

"I do."

He shrugs as he glances around his room, eyeing his vacant walls. "I think you're kind of intense, too. I mean, I know I don't know you that well, but even just standing waiting for Kara after our game, you just seemed...so serious."

"And that's why you approached me?" I ask curiously. "Something about that drew you in?"

"Not exactly."

I tilt my head. "Then why did you?"

"I just...I'm trying to live in the moment, you know?

Like I said before, I want to enjoy my life day by day. And when I came out of the locker room on a post-game high to see the hot girl with the orange hair from the stands waiting around, I just kind of went for it."

"Oh," I breathe.

"So, yeah," he continues after clearing his throat. "How about it, then? Next weekend?"

"What would we do, though?" I press. "Do we even have anything in common?"

"I'm sure we can figure something out."

As interested as I am in him, my nerves are bubbling up, and without the buffer of Kara and Charlie and all the people downstairs, the thought makes me feel a little antsy.

I've never been on an actual date before, and I'm partially convinced it would just be a lot of awkward over-analyzing on my part.

"I think we're doing just fine so far," he adds quickly as we both pick up on the sounds of Kara and Charlie bounding back up the stairs. "No harm in seeing where it goes."

I can't argue with that.

EIGHT

I'm starting to think sugar is the cure for all of life's ailments.

While I do understand that too much of it can have negative health effects, the instant a grain of it hits my tongue—regardless of whether it's baked into something or swirled in a cup of tea—it's like my brain gets an instant boost.

It's why I've chosen to have chocolate pudding as my first meal today, figuring that since it's one o'clock in the afternoon, this can serve as a fill-in for brunch.

Kara and I snuck back here in the middle of the night, ensuring I had several hours, plenty of water, and many carbohydrates between that one shot and my getting behind the wheel.

She's still in a deep sleep upstairs—no doubt the result of the additional vodka she and Charlie downed upon their return to Penn's bedroom after they'd successfully scored us all some pizza—so I'm milling about the kitchen.

I yawn as I rifle through the pantry, deciding this is the perfect day to test out some recipes for both the bake sale and my family's Thanksgiving.

It will also give me an excuse to eat many desserts.

To balance it out, though, I cut up an apple and a few stalks of celery, then drop a big blob of peanut butter on a plate, figuring I should get at least some nutrition today.

Next, I pull out the various ingredients and flours I have at my disposal.

I'm not thrilled with the lack of chocolate chips or how low the can of baking powder is getting, but I make do by starting with the holiday classic that's easy enough to warm me up for the more complicated recipes—a simple pumpkin pie.

Without having had the foresight to know this was going to be my weekend afternoon activity, I obviously don't have a crust ready in the fridge, which means I have to settle on a store-bought one hiding in the back of the freezer.

I'm definitely not a snob when it comes to this kind of stuff, but it's almost always better to go with something fresh over something with a long shelf-life. But, from experience, I know that this crust will be thicker but far less of a hassle.

I press the buttons on the oven to get it preheating, then shift my focus to making the best filling I can, hoping it will somehow compensate for the shortcut.

I double-check online that I can use evaporated milk instead of heavy cream, then start dumping the ingredients into a bowl.

The mixer that I'm pretty sure my mom got as a

wedding gift died a few months ago, which means I'm stuck mixing and whipping all the ingredients by hand. It's definitely not ideal, but I get the job done.

As soon as I slide the assembled pie into the oven, I start on the cinnamon brownies Erica specifically requested.

Some of my recipes have been tweaked from existing ones, but this is one that's wholly my own, created from nothing but me testing different flours and ingredients. The cinnamon was honestly a bit of an accident, but once I gave in and I tried it, I was hooked.

"I can't decide if finding you elbows-deep in flour after your first big party is a good sign or a bad one," Ryan says as he appears in the kitchen.

I let out a short laugh. "It's a fine one."

"Fine?" He eyes me skeptically and moves toward the coffee maker. "Not the greatest party?"

I consider his question while I use a spatula to scrape all the remnants of batter into the square pan.

"It just felt kind of...normal," I admit to him. "I didn't partake in any of the heavy *partying*. I mostly played video games, then helped clean up before we came home."

He pours the remaining coffee into a mug—which was likely made hours ago by my mom—and puts it in the microwave to heat up.

"It sounds like a win for me," Ryan says as the scent of coffee fills the air.

"For you?" I ask, quirking a brow.

He shrugs, then takes a sip. "That means we raised you right, kiddo."

"I guess you should take what you can as a parenting win."

"I will," Ryan declares with a chuckle as he sits at the table.

"But, then again, who says I didn't learn my level-headed personality and good habits for myself?"

"Me," he says pointedly. "You and your mom barely managed to put your laundry away before I came along."

"Sure, sure, take all the credit," I tease as the oven beeps.

I don mitts to shake the dish and check the consistency, then carefully pull out the picture-perfect pie.

With a smile, I place it on the cooling rack, finding immense satisfaction at the scent and sight of it. I'm dreading the time I need to wait for it to cool before I can eat it.

"That looks amazing," Ryan compliments, craning his neck to get a better look.

"Thank you," I say graciously.

He watches as I put the pan of brownies in the oven, but when I start moving the dirty dishes into the sink, he jumps up to help.

"I'll wash, you dry?"

I nod. "Sounds good. And I appreciate it."

We work quietly side by side, sharing the water from the spigot to wash the spatulas, mixing bowls, and measuring cups.

I actually don't mind the cleanup process, but it's nice to have the company.

Ryan and I find a good rhythm as the aroma of baking

cinnamon and chocolate fills the air, combining with the lemony scent of the bubbling soap.

It's oddly comforting to have him helping me while Kara sleeps and my mom and my siblings are out preoccupied.

Ryan gives the mixing bowl a final rinse, and I smile at him before drying it and putting it back in the cabinet.

"There's actually something I wanted to talk to you about," he says slowly.

His tone immediately smothers all the lightness I'm feeling.

"Yeah?" I prompt, crossing my arms as I lean against the counter.

My pose is easy, but my mind races with possible topics of discussion—college, money, my mother, who knows.

He clears his throat. "Your father got in touch with me yesterday."

That's definitely not what I expected him to say.

"What?" I say dumbly. "Why?"

Ryan rinses his hands, then flicks the water off them into the sink. "He mentioned that you never responded to his message. And your mother hasn't returned his call, so he tracked me down at the office to make sure everything is okay."

I wince, imagining the worst-case scenario—Ryan being in some big meeting or working on some important project only to be interrupted by my father.

Despite the obvious animosity that could occur between the two men, Ryan and my biological father have been cordial the few times they've crossed paths. Usually, they greet each other with a handshake, and Ryan congratulates my dad on whatever big story he's recently published.

But I should have known that being quiet for so long would mean my dad might try harder to track me down.

"I'm sorry," I say with a frown. "I hope he didn't bother you too much."

"It's fine," he says immediately. "I don't mind that, but I am a little concerned. About you. I know he hasn't been around lately, but it seems like—"

"Lately?" I interrupt. "Try *ever*."

Ryan keeps his expression neutral. "It seems like he's really eager to talk to you. He didn't say much on the phone, but I think he's hoping you'll text or call him back so you can reconnect."

"Well, good for him," I snap.

The timer goes off, and I busy myself with checking the brownies—sticking a toothpick a few inches down and making sure it comes out clean—before I set the pan beside the pumpkin pie.

It buys me a few minutes of silence, but Ryan is apparently keen to press the issue because the peace comes to an end.

"Are you avoiding him?" he asks calmly. "Is there some reason you've put him off?"

I let out a breath. "Maybe a little bit. I was definitely surprised to hear from him. I guess I haven't reached out because I don't know what to say. I don't know what he wants, and I kind of want to know that before I do. But then I'm stuck because the only way to find out is to actually *talk* to him..."

"Okay," Ryan says, nodding along as I speak.

"And the worst part is that it's so random for him to reach out, you know? Like, usually he sticks to the major holidays, but he's missed every single one of those for the past few years, so I can't figure out why I'm hearing from him now."

"And you don't want to rip off the Band-Aid and just text him and ask him about it?" Ryan presses. "Feel him out and let him know you're okay before you agree to anything else?"

"Is that what you think I should do?" I ask, genuinely seeking his advice.

He remains silent for a long moment, shifting his weight and shoving his hands into the pockets of his jeans.

It's not that Ryan isn't opinionated because he definitely is, but he is good at establishing boundaries and trying to be respectful of ones already in place.

Unlike the rest of my family.

"I just really don't want to overstep," he starts.

"Please," I practically beg. "I'm looking for advice here, so go ahead and step. Stomp, even."

We both laugh, and it brings a little relief from the heaviness of the conversation.

"Relationships of any type are never easy. But the truth is that no matter how well you know a person, no matter how informed the mental image you have of them is...you never know exactly what they're going through until you talk to them. And maybe that's all he wants, Violet. Or maybe he wants to apologize. Or maybe he's just unaware of how he's been acting and the impact it's had on you."

I let out a long exhale. "You think I should talk to him, then?"

"It's *my* preference to face things head-on," Ryan says.

"That's not what I heard from Mom," I argue with a smile. "She said that when you were dating, you were 'too coy for your own good.'"

"That's how she ruined my meticulously planned proposal, by the way," Ryan huffs. "I had a whole romantic night planned but ended up having to drop down on one knee in the middle of the kitchen because she was freaking out at how 'weird' and 'shifty' I was acting."

I have heard this story many times, of course, and don't mind using it as fodder.

But our camaraderie feels good.

I know that no matter what drama I'm dealing with from my absentee father, Ryan's going to be there for me and support me—that knowledge is backed up by the thousands of memories and moments we've already shared as a family.

"Thank you," I say to him.

He reaches for his long-forgotten mug. "Anytime, kiddo. You know I'm always here for you."

I do without a doubt.

Our moment ends just as the garage door opens, and I brace myself for the onslaught of four sets of little feet and even bigger personalities.

But only one person steps into the house.

"Mom?" I say, surprised. "Where's everyone else?"

She smiles as she puts down bags of takeout from my favorite Italian restaurant. "I got us a little late lunch treat. June is at Sophia's. Chloe is at that all-day dance event at the studio. And Kevin and The Baby are supposed to be here..."

"They are," Ryan confirms. "I heard signs of life from their bedroom not too long ago. They were watching one of the *Spider-Man* movies."

"Good," my mom says as she starts to unpack the food.

Before she can get too far, Ryan wraps his arms around her, then pulls her in for a hug and kiss on the cheek, eliciting a grin and a slight squeal.

"Precious," Kara says as she leans against the wall for support.

I didn't hear her usually heavy steps coming down the stairs, but I wouldn't be surprised if she tiptoed to eavesdrop on my conversation with Ryan.

But also, looking at how ghastly pale and disheveled she is, she could very well have spent the past hour slowly making her way into the kitchen.

"Oh my," my mom says with an amused expression. "You need some toast and aspirin."

Kara crosses the kitchen and slumps into a chair. "I do," she says as she closes her eyes. "So much aspirin."

I laugh at her expense.

"I'm assuming your experience at the party was more than just 'fine,' then?" Ryan teases.

"It was very loud," Kara groans. "I swear I can still feel the thudding at the front of my skull."

"That's a hangover," my mother says matter-of-factly before handing over a few pills and a glass of water.

Kara drops them in her mouth and drains half the glass in one go. "Thank you."

"Oh wow, Violet." My mom nods to the cooling desserts as she pulls out plates. "These look great. What's the occasion?"

"Just felt in the mood to bake." I eye Kara as I continue. "Erica asked me to make some treats for her improv club's bake sale. I thought I might as well get some practice in."

I don't know if it's the next-day effects of alcohol or something deeper, but Kara doesn't even blink as I mention my other best friend.

Which is the opposite of the slightly panicked and heavily territorial reaction that Kara's name usually elicits from Erica.

"And we get to benefit," Ryan says with a smile.

My mom nods in agreement. "How much longer until they're ready?"

"We can dig into the brownies now," I say. "If you want to eat dessert alongside that chicken parmesan."

"This should be a new Sunday tradition," Ryan says. "Takeout and treats."

"I don't hate it," I admit.

"Me neither," Kara says. "You got any breadsticks?"

I find the one with the least amount of garlic and butter, thinking that plain food is best, and put it on a plate for her.

She nods gratefully before she bites the corner, then takes her time to chew and swallow.

"You sure that's what you want?" Ryan asks warily as we all sit at the table.

Kara immediately shakes her head and pushes the plate aside. "I think I'll stick with water for now."

My mom, however, has no problem digging into her food before prying for details. "So, tell me all about last night."

"Nothing really to tell," I say.

Ryan wipes his mouth with a napkin. "Apparently there were video games and cleaning."

"How responsible of you," my mom says in amusement, twirling her pasta around her fork.

"That makes one of us," Kara mumbles.

I shrug. "That's really it."

Kara pulls her legs up onto the chair, tucking her feet in close to her butt and wrapping her arms around her knees so she's in a seated fetal position. "Did you text Penn?"

My mother's eyes widen. "Penn? Who's that?"

"Kara's teammate," I say quickly. "The party was at his house."

"And instead of being a good host and hanging with the team, he stayed glued to your side the entire night," Kara adds with a snort.

I glare at my best friend before I address the table. "He's...nice."

I know if I show too much outward excitement, it will become a big subject with my mom.

An exchange student lived next door to us during my freshman year, and when she found out I had a crush on him, she hired the poor guy to do odd chores around our house, and she did everything she could to get us in the same room together.

It was beyond embarrassing, and I don't want a repeat of it in any fashion.

"'Nice' is good," Ryan says eventually. "Jess, did you get a chance to talk to Chloe's dance teacher about spring classes?"

I'm so ridiculously grateful for his pivoting the conversation that I vow to make whatever desserts he wants next weekend as a thank you.

Kara, however, doesn't drop the subject.

"You should text him," she urges.

"Maybe," I say noncommittally.

Although my heart does a little pitter-patter at the thought of Penn, I'm not sure how I feel about him or his proposal of a date.

I choose to focus on siphoning little flakes of chocolate off the top of my brownie because desserts are far less complex than navigating people who exist in my phone waiting for me to reach out.

NINE

It takes us more than a week, but Erica and I finally make plans to hang out.

Her schedule is very complex between coordinating dates with Alex, attending Alex's games, leaving room for family time, and participating in improv club.

It all seems exhausting.

Some days, I feel like I'm barely hanging on with just school and family stuff, so I don't know how she does it all.

Actually, I guess that's why she always has to copy my homework...

But I think even when I eventually have a boyfriend, I won't prioritize him over everything else. I couldn't see myself missing The Baby's birthday or one of Kara's home games just because he wanted to hang around.

Then again, Penn would be playing in those very same home games. And given how interested he is in getting to know me, I don't think he'll mind meeting my family, let alone getting his own serving of birthday cake at—

I blink as I realize what I'm doing, then laugh at the way I've imagined him in those scenarios so easily.

"Here you go," Erica says.

I focus on the cup of tea she offers me, partially so I don't have to come to terms with what my own subconscious has revealed.

"Thanks," I say, genuinely grateful for her well-timed return and the drink.

Erica nods as she sits down with her monstrosity of whipped cream.

She wanted us to meet up at Books & Beans, which is pretty close to being equal distance from our houses, and there's the added bonus of getting to use my mom's employee discount, even though she's not here, so I'm happy.

Over the years, my mom has helped transform this space from an organized mess of coffee-stained pages to an actual storefront with seating and plenty of cute journals and bookmarks for sale.

"It's been forever since I've been in here," Erica says with a satisfied smile.

I nod, even though it's only been a few days for me.

"Are these new?" she asks.

I follow the line of her waved hand in the direction of some art pieces hung unevenly on the wall. They include a few portraits and some abstracts done in charcoal, and although I've never really been into art, I like their simplicity and style.

"Maybe?" I answer with uncertainty. "I'll have to ask my mom about it."

"She's not working today?" Erica clarifies, glancing around as if expecting her to miraculously appear.

I quirk a brow. "June has a doctor's appointment, so she cut out a little early."

Erica takes a sip from her drink, then sighs. "I wish my mom worked at a cool place like this."

It's funny to hear her say that, given that for a while I wished my mom was more like Erica's—put together, dressed in pantsuits, and without a hair out of place—instead of picking me up from science camp wearing a coffee-stained apron.

I frown at the harshness of my past self, and my change of opinion makes me wonder what I might look back on with regret in another few years.

"The only employee discount *I* can get is on taxes or accounting services or something boring," Erica continues. "Though, I guess my dad did get Alex and me those Pirates tickets over the summer."

I hum in acknowledgment, then renew my gaze on hers, realizing I haven't given her an update on what's going on with me.

"Speaking of dads," I say plainly. "Mine reached out."

Erica blinks in surprise. "Really?"

"Really," I say before taking a small sip of tea.

"What is he up to? Is he covering something dangerous? Or inspiring and perspective-altering like the piece he did on refugees a few months ago?"

I trace the handle of my mug with my fingertips. "You read that?"

"Of course I did," she says. "His work is incredible.

Don't you read it all and just sit around, completely awed that you're related to someone with that talent?"

"Not really."

She rolls her eyes. "Violet. He's one of the most important reporters overseas right now! You're his daughter, and you don't even care? I get that you're not into his job, but come on, you have to respect him for it."

"It's not that I'm not interested or impressed by what he does. I just—" I stop short, wondering why I even have to explain myself to her.

She knows just as much as my parents and Kara do that my dad is and has been largely absent—and that it has been hard on me for a number of years.

But she's overlooking it in favor of her own admiration.

And as that realization hits me, a memory jogs from the recesses of my mind of the last time I saw my dad.

It was right after I turned sixteen, and before that, it had been nearly a year since I saw him in person. I was so nervous that I asked Erica to tag along. I figured she'd be a good buffer to quell my anxiety and keep the conversation going in case there were lulls—but I had been worried for nothing.

Because I didn't have to say anything at all.

The two of them powered the conversation, talking about current events, his job, and Erica's future while I picked at my chicken caesar salad.

I didn't think anything of it at the time because I was so grateful we didn't lapse into awkward silence, but looking at the evening from my current perspective, I'm appalled.

Erica lets out a huff before she voices her impatience. "Well, at the very least, you should do it for me. I mean, I'd love to hear what he's up to. Actually, you know what? He offered to take a look at some of my reels, do you remember that?"

"No," I say flatly.

"Well, he did. I'll have to send them over so you can show him or forward them to him."

I sink my teeth into my bottom lip as her phone buzzes, grateful that the distraction saves me from having to offer her a response.

Erica smiles widely while she reads the message on her phone, then her fingers fly to type up a response.

"Alex is the *sweetest,*" she says, refocusing her gaze on me. "Look at all these pictures we took for our anniversary."

She turns her phone toward me, and I'm reluctantly led through at least twenty photos of them posing in her backyard.

The shots themselves are actually kind of nice. The two of them are framed by the fence on her property, and they look at ease with each other despite the obvious pose.

It's the type of portrait that comes in store-bought frames, smiles wide and somewhat matching clothing.

She's only able to hold my attention for so long, though, and mental fatigue surfaces as I scramble to make commentary and hum along with her explanations of every single detail.

Now that I think about it, her relationship with Alex has been this way from the beginning—flashed in my face, even though I've had no interest in it. I've wanted to be a supportive friend, despite my dislike of his character, so

I've tried to maintain enthusiasm for her gushing and over-sharing.

I've been there since the start—the first night they got together. It feels like so long ago now, but it was after the spring talent show. She performed with the improv club, and I hung out backstage to wait for her so we could carpool home.

Before we left, Alex approached her, confident as always, and asked her out.

Despite his bravado, their interactions at first were a little stilted, but I don't pick up on any of that now, in person or in these photos.

And I very selfishly wonder how they went from *that* to *this*.

"Hey, Erica," I blurt out.

She finally puts her phone down to give her attention back to her drink. "Yeah?"

"What was it like when you first started dating Alex?"

"What do you mean?" she asks, appraising me with a tilted head. "You were kind of there for it."

I withhold a grimace, recalling the moment they snuck away from our class field trip to go make out in another room of the Science Center. And worse, I had to hear about the details of their first kiss for the entirety of the bus ride back.

I clear my throat. "I know, but how did you know that he really liked you?"

"I'd say it was pretty obvious when he asked me out," Erica says on a laugh.

I can't tell if she's being evasive on purpose, but my cheeks heat in frustration and embarrassment. "That's not what I mean…it's kind of interesting to remember you and Alex going from just starting dating to where you are now."

"That's pretty sweet, actually."

I offer her a flat smile before I take another drink. "So, I kind of—"

"Oh, no," she cuts in, face falling as she looks at her screen again. "My mom wants me to come home."

"Okay," I breathe as she stands.

"She's pissed I have a C in Spanish, but she doesn't get that we're seniors and none of this really matters at this point," she says. "I doubt Northwestern is going to care about that once they see my SAT scores."

"Right."

"But, hey," she says brightly. "This was fun!"

"Definitely," I say, attempting to match her emotion.

She smiles as she grabs her bag and her coffee. "I'll see you tomorrow, okay?"

I watch as she retreats, and even after she leaves, I don't move, letting our conversation roll over me.

I wring my hands as I process all the little things I haven't noticed over the past few months—or maybe years at this point.

It's not a great feeling.

Because I've always considered Kara and Erica to have equal footing in my life, their different personalities and interests making each relationship special.

But now, instead of feeling like the bridge between them, it's like I've got two feet firmly planted in my friendship with Kara, and I'm merely hanging on the edge of Erica's.

I've just realized that while every relationship has

pushes and pulls, she's only there for me when it benefits *her*. I'm not sure if she really cares about me or if she just wants someone to be a fixture in her life.

And I think it's the exact same way with my father.

"You look like you need this."

I startle as Marie, the owner of Books & Beans and my mom's boss, dangles a chocolate bar in front of me.

A genuine sigh of relief surfaces as she drops it in my palm.

I've known Marie for years, even before she hired my mom to work for her full-time.

She's one of the nicest, most observant people I've ever met—and not just because she gives me sweets when I'm stressing over homework or recovering from emotional whiplash. I've seen her casually interrupt awkward silences between couples and nudge someone into reading a book they didn't even know they needed.

"You okay?" Marie asks.

I nod and tap the treat with my fingertips. "I am now. Thank you."

"Good." She gathers Erica's trash before I can wave her off. "And you know, if you need an objective third party, who is not a boyfriend-obsessed friend or your parents, to hear you out about whoever's on your mind, I'm happy to do so."

"I appreciate it," I tell her.

But I don't take her up on it.

At this moment, I don't think I need anyone else's advice. If anything, I'm overloaded with everyone else's opinions.

I just want to do something for myself.

Once Marie is back behind the counter, I pull my phone out of my bag, then I scroll through my list of contacts until I land on Penn.

He saved himself as "Penn Westbrook aka Blue (But Should Be Violet) Yoshi."

I smile genuinely for the first time since I sat down, then open a new message. Before I can overthink what I'm doing, I send the first thing that comes to my mind.

Hi. It's Violet.

It's only after the message shows as delivered that I frown at how boring an introduction that is.

Nothing I can do about it, though, so I stare out the window as I take small and deliberate bites of the milky chocolate bar, then jump when my phone goes off a moment later.

I thought you forgot about me.

I wonder if that means he's been thinking of me, too.

Another message arrives, sparing me from trying to decide how to address the first one.

But I suppose I might be unforgettable...you know, with the charming persona going on.

I let out a little laugh. *Charming?*

Absolutely.

I don't know about that. I can think of some other descriptions.

Like what? Penn asks.

Intense. I reply, thinking of what we talked about in person. *And maybe a little self-aggrandizing...*

There's a pause before he responds. *I had to look up that last one.*

The wonders of Google.

Yeah. Well, I'm not sure if I agree with your assessment.

I send him the shrugging emoji.

Oh, we're doing emojis now? Wow. Already at that stage. I mean, look at us, Violet. We're doing it.

My brows pinch. *Doing what?*

Having a conversation when you said we had nothing in common.

I let out a sigh. *I guess you're right.*

So, about that offer I made of seeing you again…do I take these texts as a sign that you're up for it?

I pause and close my eyes, trying to imagine his expression.

I can sense the humor in his words, but I wonder if he's squirming each time my response comes through like I am with his—or if he's tugging on the ends of his hair in anticipation like I saw him do a few times at the party.

My phone vibrates again, and I open my eyes to see a new message, but it's not from Penn.

It's Kara.

AM I SNOOPING OVER PENN'S SHOULDER ON THIS STUPID LONG BUS RIDE TO OUR AWAY GAME TO SEE THAT HE IS NOT ONLY TEXTING YOU BUT TRYING TO GET YOU TO GO ON A DATE WITH HIM???????

I shake my head at her screamy text but immediately reply. *Yes.*

IS THAT YES SUPPOSED TO GO TO ME OR HIM?

I don't get time to answer her question before she texts again.

DO IT DO IT DO IT!!!

As much as I just mentally declared that I don't want to hear more opinions or go along with what anyone else tells me to do, in this case, the outcome would be the same if I made the choice myself.

I pull up Penn's chat again. *How about this Saturday?*

Done. Can I pick you up at eight?

Yes. I respond, then drop a pin of my address.

When he sends back a little purple heart, all I can do is swoon at the sight.

TEN

I think "date" is such a strange word.

It feels sort of antiquated, but it's the term Kara uses repeatedly—and with emphasis—as she helps me get ready.

She's insisted on coming over for moral support as I prepare to "hang out," which is my preferred description, with Penn, and she's entirely too amused by my nervous fidgeting.

It's not the scenario that has me feeling off-kilter or the idea of being alone with Penn.

It's the unknown.

I don't mind a little guessing when it comes to multiple choice questions or tweaking recipes, but when it comes to people, I like them to be predictable.

But then again, considering my relationship with my father and now Erica, as well as the random bursts of energy from four siblings, I guess hoping for that might be out of the realm of my actual reality.

Still, I have years of experience navigating the relationships with my friends and family, so in a way, I have a pre-formed and inherent hypothesis of how things are going to go with them.

But with Penn, I have nothing.

"So, you have no idea what the plans are?" Kara asks as she sprays the ends of my now-curled hair. "No hints dropped or anything?"

I shake my head. "He just texted me yesterday to make sure we were still on for tonight."

"Hmm."

"And we don't really have anything in common, which is exactly what I said at the party, and that makes this even more up in the air."

Kara lets out a laugh. "That's not true."

"It kind of is," I argue.

"You have *me* in common."

I roll my eyes. "You're obviously my favorite topic in the entire world—"

"As expected," she says, fluttering her hands out like she's a showgirl. "But yeah, I don't think it would be a good idea to talk about me for six hours."

"You think this is going to go on for *six hours*?" I sputter.

"I guess we'll see," she says nonchalantly. "But you could probably fill a few of them with stories from us growing up."

I let out a huff, then carefully strip off my t-shirt and pull on the long-sleeved gray sweater we already picked out. From the front, it's not anything special, but it has a criss-cross detail on the back that makes me feel a little risqué.

Kara appraises me as I smooth my black jeans and slide on a bracelet and some earrings.

"Penn is a really good guy," she says softly.

I turn to take in her gentle expression. "I know. Or rather, I hope."

She purses her lips. "But I'll kill him if he hurts you."

"I appreciate it, though I don't think it'll be necessary," I tell her.

"But just in case, know I could probably injure him at practice and make it look like an accident. One slash of a stick between his—"

"Hey, Violet?" my mom calls from the other side of my door.

And, of course, she does that whole "knock as she opens it" thing.

I bite back my annoyance. "Yeah?"

"Are you—"

She stops abruptly as we take each other in.

If there's one definitive trait I've inherited from my mother, it's being a total homebody.

I'd much rather stay in and curl up with a blanket on the couch than do most other things, and she's the same way when she's not at work or running all around town, dropping my siblings off for their various activities.

As a result, I think she and I have more pairs of sweat-pants and comfortable old shirts than any other item of clothing.

But instead of her usual Saturday night attire of leggings and a fuzzy pullover, she's wearing a form-fitting black dress.

It's stunning on her, of course, and she's even taken

time to orchestrate her hair into some sort of updo and put on red lipstick, which I don't think I've seen her do in years.

"You look great," I tell her immediately.

"Thank you," my mom says.

"*Why* do you look great?" I ask, voicing my confusion.

She laughs and eyes me curiously. "I could ask you the same question. You look awfully dressed up to babysit tonight."

"What?" I balk.

Kara appears beside me as if she can sense my inner panic.

My mom's forehead wrinkles. "Tonight is that casino night event. Marie gave Ryan and me tickets to go to the fundraiser downtown, remember? The one for the food bank she donates her leftovers to?"

"I don't remember this," I say, slightly panicked.

"We asked you weeks ago if you'd babysit for us tonight."

I shake my head adamantly. "No, you asked me if I'd babysit on the nineteenth."

"Yes," she says slowly. "Which is today."

I blink. "No."

"Yikes," Kara mumbles.

"It is," my mom insists, finding humor in my surprise. "We already transferred the money into your account. You said you would be using it to buy—"

"The supplies for the bake sale," I interrupt.

"Oh shit," Kara says, piecing together what I've just discovered.

"No, no, no," I mutter as I breeze by my mother.

I rush down the stairs and over to the pantry, then let out a groan.

I still haven't been to the store since I made the pumpkin pie and brownies the other weekend, and my stores are totally depleted. Aside from all the specific ingredients I need, there's not even enough flour to make one batch of cookies, let alone the other treats I have planned.

Kara, who apparently followed me, pats my back reassuringly. "We'll figure it out."

"Figure what out?" Ryan asks.

He looks absurdly dapper as he enters the kitchen with my mom on his arm, and while he seems to be feeling light and excited, Mom still appears generally confused.

Kara, knowing my house just as well as I do, opens the junk drawer with a flourish. "Violet's about to have a level-ten meltdown."

"Why?" Ryan asks, concerned.

"She has to make, like, a billion baked goods," she explains as she pulls out a notepad and a pen. "And she forgot about it because she's been so focused on her date."

"A date?" Ryan repeats.

My mom's eyes widen in understanding. "That's why you're all dressed up."

Kara hands me the pen. "Write down what you want, and I'll go get it for you."

It's really kind of her to offer, but I don't even know exactly what I want to make yet.

And I'll need some time to work out the quantity, double the recipes, and see what ingredients overlap...

"You had a *date* planned for tonight, and you didn't say

anything about it?" my mom asks with both hurt and surprise in her tone.

"It's not a big deal," I say dismissively.

She scoffs. "Not a big deal?"

I shrug. "Penn and I were just going to hang out."

And now I have to cancel on him last minute, which is pretty crappy of me.

I reach into my pocket to pull out my phone only to realize that I left it upstairs.

My mom steps in front of me and blocks my path before I can scurry out. "So, you were just going to go out—"

"Well, it doesn't seem like it's going to happen now, so maybe we can save this for later," Ryan says impatiently as he checks his watch. "We don't want to be late."

"Violet is close enough with a boy to go on a *date* with him, and you just want to carry on with our evening?" she fires back.

"Yes," my stepdad says immediately. "It's been forever since we went out, and I think we'll get the same non-answers whether you press for them now or tomorrow morning. If it's okay with you, I'd like to show off my gorgeous wife for a few hours outside the house."

My mom blushes and, thankfully, doesn't argue.

"The kids are all upstairs playing peacefully," Ryan tells me as he grabs his keys from the bowl. "Enjoy the quiet while you can."

But the doorbell rings just as they step toward the door that leads to the garage, and my mom brings them to a halt.

"Guh," I groan.

"You can go out for a few hours while I watch the others," Kara suggests. "Go enjoy yourself."

I shake my head as she follows me toward the entryway. "I have too much to do. I won't be able to think about anything else the entire time."

"Violet," Kara scolds, pushing me along. "It's all going to be fine. Enjoy yourself and deal with the pastry problems later."

I open the door without any finesse and immediate realize that while I knew what was going to happen tonight, I am not at all prepared to see Penn standing on my front step.

"Violet," he says brightly.

And I instantly warm at the sight of him.

He's definitely put more care into his appearance than the last time I saw him.

His hair is slicked back slightly, and he's wearing a button-down shirt untucked, though it's partly obscured by a little potted plant he holds in his hands.

"Is that a succulent?" Kara asks, stepping forward.

Penn's mouth twitches at the corners as he tilts his head. "Kara?"

"Surprise!" She does some sort of jazz hands movement. "Happy first date!"

He lets out a laugh. "Thank you."

I open my mouth to try and explain the situation, but I'm at a momentary loss for words.

"Come in," Kara invites Penn, tugging me backward.

He quirks a brow at me, silently asking permission, and I wave him in.

"You look pretty," he murmurs to me.

"Thank you," I say, feeling my cheeks flush at his appraisal.

"We're heading out," Ryan calls as he helps my mom into her jacket.

"Just wait," my mom shoos him away as her eyes widen at our new addition. "Hi!"

Penn awards her and Ryan a very charming smile. "Hello."

Kara nudges me, then gives a pointed look.

"Right." I clear my throat. "Mom, Ryan, this is Penn."

He immediately reaches out to shake their hands. "It's really nice to meet you both," he says kindly. "I'm here to take Violet out."

"Is that a succulent?" Ryan asks good-naturedly.

"Oh, yeah." Penn lets out a low chuckle. "My grandma told me I should bring flowers, but I feel like that's kind of rude, you know? Like, if I bring them, you have to cut them and find a vase. It's a whole thing just to watch something beautiful die. So, I went the low-maintenance route."

My mother legitimately squeals at his explanation.

"That is very…thoughtful of you, Penn," Ryan tells him.

"I try," he returns, then makes a show of offering it to me.

"Thank you." I take the pot from him and set it on the windowsill by the sink. "This is very unnecessary but very sweet."

"I do what I can," Penn says.

"Well, we've *really* got to be off," Ryan says, placing a firm hand on my mother's lower back. "Call us if the house is on fire."

From the way my mom's eyes flit between Penn and me,

it's obvious she wants to stick around and ask more questions, but she allows Ryan to lead her out.

"Behave yourselves," Kara says as they walk toward the garage.

Ryan turns and winks. "Not planning on it."

My mom hits him with her clutch, then they officially leave us.

I let out a breath, glad we've successfully overcome the first hurdle of the evening—even though I know my mom is going to lead an inquisition tomorrow.

"What's all this?" Penn asks, gesturing to the mess of ingredients on the counter.

"It's…" I trail off and sigh. "I'm so sorry, Penn."

He quirks a brow. "For what?"

"I have to cancel on you tonight."

"Wait, why?"

"I totally forgot I have to babysit tonight, which would be fine since Kara volunteered to stay…except I promised my friend Erica I'd bake all these desserts for the bake sale this week. And I don't have any of the ingredients. I also didn't plan out what to make when, and it's a mess now… though if I switch to apple pie, it'll stay good for a few days refrigerated if no one cuts into it. And I guess I could make some dough for plain gingerbread cookies, but those aren't really Thanksgiving-y treats, which is what Erica was hoping for."

Kara lets out a low snort. "How did you manage to say that all in one breath?"

But Penn doesn't blink. "What exactly do you need?"

It shouldn't be a surprise that he maintains a cool head

under pressure—though, admittedly, the pressure is solely mine—but I appreciate it.

"I have to bake a bunch of things before Tuesday," I explain. "But first, I need to go get supplies, like flour and butter and sugar and other stuff."

Penn's gaze moves from the notepad to me. "Well, it's a good thing I've got a full tank of gas, and there are many grocery stores within a twenty-mile radius."

I don't bother biting back a smile.

ELEVEN

I read over my list for the tenth time as we enter through the automatic doors, quickly doing the multiplication and running through the steps to ensure I haven't missed anything.

I probably have, though, because as sweet and patient as Penn is, he's also very distracting.

On the way here, he quietly listened to nineties rock music and tapped out the beat on the steering wheel while I scribbled away, but I stole occasional glances at him, and he caught me more than once.

Now, I have to put the physical barrier of a shopping cart between us just to give myself something else to focus on when all I want to do is stand and stare at him.

"Should we start here?" Penn asks as we enter the produce section.

"We?" I tease.

"Well, yeah. I have my own list of stuff to buy, and

while this is not exactly what I pictured for our first date, I might as well be productive."

"Might as well," I agree as curiosity takes over. "What *did* you have planned?"

Penn looks a little sheepish. "Just dinner and a movie. Which I know is kind of boring. But I thought we could use our palates and media preferences to discover some more common ground."

"It was a good plan," I compliment him as I grab a compostable bag.

"We're on a similar course of action now, though," Penn says, reaching for his own. "I mean, we are technically surrounded by food."

"I don't consider apples to be a suitable dinner."

Penn nods as he inspects the fruit to make sure the skin is unmarred. "Probably for the best."

"Although, this girl in my class, Emily, did an apple cleanse once," I recall, placing my selection in the cart.

"An apple cleanse?"

"Yep." I shake my head at the memory of how miserable she looked. "She ate, like, six apples over the course of a day."

"That's...wow," Penn says with a laugh.

"Ridiculous?" I offer. "But also kind of impressive. I mean, she really put in effort to make that many apples appealing. She sliced some and peeled others. One she ate whole, even the core."

"I didn't know you could eat the core," Penn says. "Did she stick to all the same kind?"

"I think she had a mix of red and green ones before breaking down and eating an entire pizza."

"Is that your preference, too? A variety of apples? Minus the whole 'cleanse' part."

"I guess."

"Well, I notice you've selected Granny Smith and Honeycrisp as your choices today."

"Yes."

Penn looks stupidly adorable as he takes over to steer the cart, leaning his elbows on the handle as we continue our slow movement through the produce section.

"Are they your favorites?" The look of incredulity I give him must not be flattering because he smiles and adds, "Humor me, Violet."

I let out a breath. "For general apple consumption, no."

"And yet you want them in a pie?"

"I just know they'll be fine in the oven," I explain. "A very bad experience taught me that Gala apples and high heat do not mix."

"Gotcha," he says. "I should let you know that I'm a Red Delicious champion. They're my favorite."

"Not a bad choice."

As I bag up a few lemons, he puts a bunch of bananas in the cart, and I frown.

If we continue on this way, slowly moving around each other and dropping our items in wherever they fall, soon our hauls will be indistinguishable.

"Penn, you can't just mix everything together," I tell him, rearranging things to create a clear line of separation between our items.

"Why not?" he counters. "I know what I've got, and you know what you got."

"But we'll have to sort everything out at checkout," I argue.

"Good thing we have our lists, then, to keep it straight," Penn says, holding up his phone.

I shake my head. "How do we know we don't have any overlap?"

Without missing a beat, he hands over his phone so I can read what he's got.

1. Bananananas
2. THE GOOD BROWN BREAD WITH THE SEEDS
3. Salsa but not the spicy green kind like last time because I still haven't recovered from the heat level despite the very unassuming and very distinguished gentleman smiling up at me on the label
4. Can o' corn
5. Paste Of The Teeth

"What is this?" I ask as the laughter bubbles up.

"My list," he says seriously. "I have an ongoing note for all the random things Nana or I mention between our trips to the store."

"Nana? You live with your grandmother?"

He nods as we start walking again. "And she's very particular about her brand of toothpaste, so I even took a picture of it to make sure I don't mess it up."

"Don't you mean *Paste Of The Teeth*?" I deadpan. "Besides, you've already veered off course with your apple choice. A Red Delicious is not on either of our lists."

"Allow me," Penn says, taking his phone back to add another item.

6. Reddy delly apple-y

"That's absurd," I say, but I can't hide my amused snicker.

"Maybe a little bit," Penn concedes. "But I think the best things in life are."

I wouldn't be human if I didn't let those words affect me, but I'm sure there's a very dreamy expression on my face that I hide away by turning toward the next aisle.

We move through all the rows of dry goods, comparing preferences and slowly building up a mountain of purchases in the cart until I bring us to a halt in the baking aisle.

Something about seeing all the beautiful, prepackaged kits along with the separate ingredients and decorating supplies makes me a little giddy.

"Have you always liked to bake?" Penn asks, watching me read the labels.

"Sort of," I answer. "I think most people have good memories in the kitchen, so it's natural to appreciate the nostalgia of the moment that a parent let you lick the spoon of batter or you helped yourself to icing...and to want to recreate that feeling."

"Is it like that for you?"

"It's definitely rewarding to create something I can enjoy after," I explain. "But really, it's the science of it all."

"Says the future meteorologist," Penn says flippantly before it hits him, and he renews his gaze on me. "Well, now that makes sense."

I nod. "It's a pretty low-stakes science experiment. For instance, I've learned it makes a big difference if you add or subtract flour and if you refrigerate the dough before you bake it."

"Interesting."

"What about you?" I ask as I continue dropping items into the cart. "What kind of things do you like?"

"Aside from you, you mean?" Penn teases.

"I'm not a *thing*," I immediately protest.

He barks out a laugh. "I know. Let's see…uh, you know I like video games. And hockey. And I guess there's really not much more to it. Which is probably your biggest fear because I'm a total conversation-stopper at this moment."

"Well, to your point, we seem to be doing just fine," I admit begrudgingly. "Even though we're majorly delaying all my prep work."

I glance at the endcap of the aisle, ensuring I'm not missing anything that's on sale, then immediately scowl at the sight before me.

"Oh, no," I groan. "They already have the Christmas stuff out."

"You say that like it's a bad thing." Penn walks toward one of the displays. "I love the holidays."

"It's not even Thanksgiving yet," I argue. "I'm not ready to see Santa."

"But just look at all these different candy canes," Penn says gleefully. "This one is *Funfetti* flavored, Violet. I didn't even know they made all these kinds, let alone with the best cake flavor around."

I smile at his excitement. "You know, I feel like I should be offended by that statement. You haven't tasted one of *my* cakes yet."

"Sorry," Penn replies immediately. "If that offends your

sensibilities, I'll just get these ones that are supposed to taste like Sweetarts."

"Get what you want but just add it to your list," I say playfully.

He tosses the box into the cart, then types it into his phone. "Done."

Grinning, I lead us to the refrigerated section, and once there, I grab butter and milk, then check the dozen eggs in a carton before I place it in the cart.

"Did you know that in other parts of the world, they don't refrigerate eggs?" I say conversationally.

He shakes his head. "Really?"

"Apparently, they can stay at room temperature as long as they have always been at said temperature," I explain, recalling the article I read a few months ago. "But since we Americans refrigerate them at one point, we have to continue to do so or they'll breed bacteria."

"What if it's really cold outside?" Penn presses. "If a British chicken lays an egg in freezing temperatures, do they have to maintain that level of coldness?"

"A valid question," I muse. "But one I don't have the answer to. Besides, I think it's your turn."

"To share some of my nonexistent knowledge about food safety?"

I shake my head. "To answer a question I have about you."

Penn rubs his hands together in anticipation. "Shoot."

"Okay, well, I don't believe that hockey and video games are all there is to you. What else do you like?"

He considers my words. "I like horror movies. The ones

from the eighties that are kind of cringe-worthy but also fun to watch."

"Not me." I bite my lip. "I don't like anything that makes me nervous. What about your favorite food?"

"Macaroni and cheese," he says promptly, grabbing a box off the shelf as we breeze by.

"If you're thinking we should make that when we get back to my house, we might as well get a few boxes," I tell him.

He brightens as he drops three more in the cart. "That enough?"

"Yes, but I should get another gallon of milk to be on the safe side."

As we swing back through the holiday section, I also grab a roll of premade cookies with little turkeys on them.

"Wow," Penn drawls. "I assumed you were a snob about baking from scratch. I didn't take you for a cheater."

"Oh, I get these so my siblings will leave the fancy homemade stuff alone," I say. "It's a distraction technique."

"Makes sense. But I also love these kind because even someone like me won't mess them up."

"Sometimes it's just easier to take shortcuts," I admit.

We approach the final section of the store—the health and wellness products—and Penn immediately seeks out his grandmother's preferred brand of toothpaste.

"Got it," he announces, holding up the box proudly.

"Your side," I remind him as he places it in the cart.

"Done. Now, Violet. Movies. Your favorite. Go."

"I don't really watch a lot of them of my own accord. My siblings always have those annoying singalong movies on. Ryan watches a lot of sports ones. And my mom loves romances." I shrug as we walk past an impressive selection of cotton swabs. "What's your favorite season?"

"Winter," he says. "For obvious, hockey-related reasons. Yours?"

"Summer. Because the clouds are usually the most prominent then." I laugh and shake my head. "See? Nothing in common."

"Opposites attract, Violet," Penn says flippantly. "You might be a woman of science, but I'm a man of chemistry, and I know it to be true."

"I think you mean physics," I retort, ignoring his double meaning.

He winks as we turn down the hair care aisle. "Well, here we are."

"You in the market for a new shampoo?" I ask, taking in all the neatly organized items.

"I believe you promised to dye my hair," Penn says a little too proudly. "I want the true violet, though, even if I had to be blue Yoshi."

I eye him skeptically. "Are you serious?"

"I'm a man of my word. And when I said it, I meant it." He pauses as he glances down at the cart. "But I know you have a lot going on right now, so maybe we could save this activity for our second date? If you'll have me, that is."

I surprise myself at how easily I answer. "Absolutely."

TWELVE

"Welcome home!" Kara calls, jumping up from the couch.

I heave a heavy bag on the counter at the same time Penn easily drops three full grocery bags beside it.

I suppose that's another perk of going on a date with someone I don't have anything in common with—his physical strength makes up for my pathetic lack thereof.

And as a result, he's spared me multiple trips to and from the car.

"It was a roaring success," Penn tells Kara proudly.

"Looks like it. Did you happen to get any din—" She stops when I pull out the boxes of macaroni and cheese, and her eyes widen. "Nice."

"And…" I pause for emphasis as I root around in another bag to pull out her favorite protein bar. "Here."

She beams as she rips it from my hand. "Thank you! I'm starving."

"Then that will tide you over until I can get unpacked and situated," I say.

"I can help," Penn offers. "If you tell me where the pot is, I'll start boiling the water for dinner, then you can work on all the baking stuff."

I smile graciously. "Works for me. Cookware is in that cabinet. I think you might need both of those pots, though."

Penn moves, then attentively reads the back of the box and measures out the perfect amount of water.

Kara clears her throat, then gives me an amused look at how I've been ignoring my unloading duties in favor of watching Penn.

I drop my awed expression and start putting away what needs to be refrigerated, and, unfortunately, I'm not at it long before I hear thundering on the stairs.

"Oh, here we go," I groan.

Penn glances at me. "What?"

"Missile incoming," Kara tells him.

"Viiiiolet!" June's voice carries down before she ultimately makes her appearance. "Can we have—"

My sister stops moving the second she notices Penn, and her entire face scrunches up in confusion. "Who are you?"

"Don't be rude," I warn her.

"I'm not being rude," she retorts, raising her chin defiantly. "I'm just wondering who this *stranger* is in our kitchen."

"This is Kara's teammate, Penn," I explain, unsure if it's even worth getting into the details of why he's here.

Judging by his wide smile in her direction, he's not offended by the title I've given him.

"And you must be June," he surmises.

I swear he's memorized every little detail I've ever told him, and the fact that he cares so deeply without even really *knowing* me makes me like him even more.

"Yes," she admits.

"I really like your hair," he tells her. "Violet's going to do mine like yours on our next date."

"Date?" June repeats.

But instead of looking to me for my reaction, my sister looks to Kara, who nods.

June inches forward until she can lean on the counter, gripping the edge so she can lift herself up and let her feet dangle for a second or two. "And thank you," she says to Penn.

"You're welcome," he beams at her before adjusting the heat of the burners.

"Penn is the captain of my hockey team," Kara tells her.

Her eyes widen. "The captain?"

"Yeah," he says with a laugh. "You play?"

June shakes her head. "Dad and I watch the Penguins sometimes."

"She has a Lemieux jersey that's older than she is," Kara adds.

"But Kara is my favorite player!" my sister exclaims.

"Hell yes I am." Kara winks at her. "And because of that, you have my full permission to someday hock my autographs to pay for college."

Penn's jaw drops in mock-offense. "But you haven't even seen *me* play yet. Maybe I'm your new favorite."

She lets out a giggle and shakes her head. "No way."

"Just hold off on deciding until you've come to one of

our games," Penn pleads as he pours the dried noodles into the boiling water.

She shrugs, but I don't miss the gleam in her eye.

"Are those the dinosaur macaronis?" June asks, sliding over to inspect his work.

He nods. "You hungry?"

"Yes," June says. "So are the twins."

"Kevin and Chloe should be down any minute," Kara supplies. "They were getting dressed after their baths, but The Baby is already asleep."

I smile gratefully. "Thank you."

Kara pulls out the premade holiday cookies. "You can reward a job well done by baking *these*."

"I'll do it," June offers.

"Go ahead," I encourage. "Make sure you read the back first, though."

She rolls her eyes but does as I say. "Preheat the oven to three hundred and fifty degrees."

As soon as she turns on the oven, the four of us work in tandem.

Penn expertly prepares dinner. June rearranges the cookies multiple times on the sheet before finally sticking them in the oven. Kara helps me get everything organized so I can start rolling out the dough that will eventually become pie crusts.

I reach a good stopping point by the time Penn announces that dinner's ready, and June moves the cookies onto a cooling rack, which is timed perfectly with the arrival of the twins.

They immediately take a liking to Penn, but although I now firmly believe in his wonder and charm, I think they're just so excited to have food ready and waiting for them that they would have accepted bowls from a mass murderer.

I do, however, have to corral them to eat at the table instead of on the living room floor.

But as we all dig in, I find that, for once, I don't mind the chaos of the kitchen.

After we've all polished off Penn's boxed pasta and June's baked goods, Penn insists on sticking around to help me clean up. It's sweet and unnecessary, but appreciated—especially since Kara insists on doing story time and getting the kids ready for bed.

I can't tell if she is trying to avoid chores or simply giving me some time alone with Penn—I suspect the latter.

"That was fun," he says as he dries his hands on a dish towel.

"Not exactly the dinner and movie you had planned, though," I wager.

"Well, it was kind of a win for me, honestly. Had we gone to the movies, we would have just sat beside each other in silence for two hours and not really gotten to talk. Or bake."

I grin. "That's another thing we can agree on."

"What, that baking is better than sitting?" Penn teases.

"No." I shake my head. "That movies should be watched in silence. I *hate* when people talk over what's happening."

"That's good to know. Does the same rule apply at home where you can pause or wait for commercials?"

"I wish it did," I admit. "I don't think I've ever watched anything at home without being interrupted."

"You're lucky, you know."

"What do you mean?"

He exhales as he leans against the counter. "You have a family who loves you...and you're never bored, that's for sure."

I tilt my head as I assess him. "It's just you, isn't it? No siblings?"

"No siblings." Penn drops my gaze briefly and runs his hand through his hair, digging his fingers into the back of his neck before our eyes meet again. "No parents."

I frown at this revelation. "Is...is that why you live with your grandmother?"

He nods. "My parents died when I was eight. Car crash on the way to pick me up from practice."

I get the sense from his body language and his somewhat stilted delivery that it's not exactly easy for him to talk about.

He's done it, though, and I take it as a sign that whatever this is between us is moving from light and fun into something deeper and more meaningful.

That realization is as lovely as it is terrifying.

"I'm so sorry," I say, voice barely above a whisper.

He smiles sadly, then shakes his head. "Dead parents really put a damper on the whole vibe, don't they?"

I laugh quietly as I step toward him, surprising myself as I reach for his hand, finding it natural, not nerve-wracking, to do so.

And the gesture makes him grin, which is worth pushing through any lingering nervousness.

On top of all the memories I have in this space, all the fights with my siblings and the long talks with Ryan and my mom, I now get to catalog a new one.

Not just this night with Penn or the moment June offered him her favorite glass to drink out of or even this conversation, necessarily, but this feeling I have inside me.

I'm finally able to recognize it for what it is—the buzz of anticipation of what's to come.

And I want to face it head-on.

I've collected information about him and started building a mental picture about who I think he is, and while he's made his intentions clear, I'm finally starting to accept that it could be *real*.

"Penn."

He quirks a brow. "Violet."

"I'm starting to really like you."

"I know." Penn grins at me. "I knew it before you did."

I let out a chuckle. "Never mind. I take it back."

"You can't," he retorts. "It's too late. I've got you now."

I think he might be right.

THIRTEEN

I sink my teeth into the buttery rosemary focaccia bread I made, sighing happily as I chew.

Despite the frantic prepping and baking session I've been working through the past few days, I'm grateful I was able to sneak this savory snack in between baking batches of pie crusts and cookie dough.

"You're in a good mood today," Aksa says as she sits down across from me.

Her eyes are bright, and her eyebrows are raised slightly, waiting for some sort of explanation.

"Good focaccia," I say flippantly.

She gives me a look of disbelief before she gets to work readying her own lunch for consumption, which in this case means slathering an obscene amount of ketchup on her crispy chicken sandwich.

Erica glances up from copying my homework briefly. "You didn't bring any for me to sell tonight."

I'm glad that I've just taken another bite so I don't have to come up with something to say to that.

"I'm sure you'll do fine with the eight containers of other stuff Violet hauled in for you," Aksa says, tone light.

Erica shrugs before she turns back to calculus.

I nod at Aksa appreciatively, then swallow before I speak. "Any fun plans for break?"

"No," she says. "But I'm glad, honestly. I need some time to recover from last weekend. Emily and I went to the mall and the movies on Saturday, then my parents and I had a big family brunch with all my cousins. I spent the rest of my time working on my poetry project."

"Ugh," Erica groans. "I haven't even started that yet."

"Me either," Emily chimes in as she joins.

"I assume you have your project done, Violet?" Aksa says.

I shake my head. "Actually, no."

Erica's attention snaps up to mine. "*Really*? I'm legitimately shocked."

"It's not due until Monday," Aksa reminds us. "Plenty of time."

"But you're always ahead on your stuff." The nonchalance in Erica's tone is so forced it's almost funny. "I'm surprised."

I level my gaze at her. "Well, I've been busy baking nonstop for the good of the improv club."

At least she has the good sense to look a little embarrassed. "Right. Well, I offered to come help."

I bite back the comment that, no, she actually didn't.

"But I'm just *swamped* with everything going on," Erica continues. "And I'm behind on that other project for—"

"It's all good," I say, tone clipped.

Erica smiles. "Great," she says, moving back to copying my homework.

"You can take a look at my stuff if you want," Aksa offers to me. "I know you don't love English, but it's actually not a bad assignment. I hear the other class has to do a whole presentation on their analysis, but we just have to write a paper."

"It's okay," I say gratefully. "I already have the poem picked out and have an idea of what I want to write. I just need to sit down and actually do it."

"I don't think this is right," Erica says, sliding my own work back to me. "Take a look at number seven."

"Erica," I say slowly. "You do this almost every single day."

Her brows pinch. "What?"

"You think that one of my answers is wrong and call me out, and then I look at it for two seconds and tell you that I'm still correct."

"Wow," she drawls, eyes widening. "Someone's in a mood."

"I'm just telling the truth." I take another bite of my bread, wondering if I should use the hall pass I've been saving to escape to the library, but given that lunch is halfway over, I think it'd be a waste.

"Whatever," Erica sighs.

Emily carries on like nothing's amiss, dragging Aksa into a conversation about some period drama she's binge-watching on Netflix, and I sit quietly as Erica finishes with my worksheet.

I frown as I put the paper away, not liking the feeling of being trapped in this routine.

I didn't have any grand expectations for my senior year, but I guess I thought it'd be light and full of fun, and I'd be creating memories to last a lifetime.

Instead, I'm coming to terms with the fact that the changes over the past few months are too much to ignore.

For a while, I was too preoccupied with thoughts of my future and slogging through senior year coursework, but within days of meeting Penn, everything changed.

Because how good he's been to me with us not knowing each other for that long has caused my perspective to shift on the other relationships in my life.

It's like I've woken up to reality.

"What's up, beautiful ladies?" Alex calls as he approaches our table, flanked by two of his teammates.

They all claim the remaining vacant seats and immediately dive into the details of their next game—which, of course, is against Greene, the team that Kara and Penn play for.

They're not direct rivals, but from what I understand from Kara, there have been enough close games between the two that there's no love and friendship waiting for them on the ice.

"Their defense is weak, but they've been piling up goals this season," a guy named Matt says.

"Nothing we can't handle," Alex returns confidently. "I mean, you're like twice the size of their new *goalie.*"

The guys laugh a little too long, and I know exactly what they mean even if they don't say it outright.

Erica glances at me, and I clench my molars, wondering

if she's going to come to Kara's defense—or say anything at all.

"Maybe she'll be too busy checking her nail polish to notice a puck flying right at her," Alex jokes.

Matt scoffs. "Can you imagine having a *girl* on the team?"

"That's enough," I snap.

Alex lets out a jovial chuckle. "Oh, come on. We're just trash talking."

"I know," I say coldly. "I can hear you."

My phone buzzes, giving me an out from paying attention to this conversation any longer.

I suppose I could have just tuned them out or attempted to pull Aksa into a side chat of our own, but I'm grateful for the reprieve from having to actually *look* at any of the people surrounding me.

Instead, I give myself over to the flutters of excitement in my stomach at the thought of who has likely texted me.

It's not the actual message I'm excited about but the intent—I imagine Penn sitting with his friends at lunch, or whatever class he's in now, and thinking about me enough to reach out and tell me so.

But when I look at the screen, I find something even worse than my present situation.

Violet. Please call me. -Dad

I squeeze my eyes shut for a second, letting waves of disappointment, sadness, and anger roll over me before I aggressively shove my phone back in my pocket.

The only person at the table who picks up on my reaction is Aksa, and thankfully, the bell rings before she can ask what has me stressed.

FOURTEEN

I thought about this moment all day yesterday.

It was a normal Thanksgiving with football and lots of cooking and baking, but I was also distracted enough to burn the rolls I'd made from scratch and pour too much sugar in the cranberry sauce.

Because I haven't heard from Penn at all since our date, only getting updates about him through the sly details Kara dropped yesterday when I talked to her on the phone, and I'm not sure what this means.

I'm well aware that I could have picked up my phone at any time and sent him a message, but by the time I gathered up the courage to reach out, it felt awkward to just randomly text him.

It's laughable that I felt that way about one measly message, but I've somehow talked myself into the idea that walking up the path to his front door is the right move.

I just figure it's my turn to make a gesture.

"Here goes nothing," I mutter as I ring the doorbell.

It's silent for long enough that I consider adding a knock or another ring, but as I move forward to do just that, I hear shuffling inside.

I smooth my hair and put what I hope is a natural smile on my face.

When the door opens, I brace myself for Penn's easy grin and surprised eyes, but I'm greeted by an older woman who I can only assume is his grandmother.

Her gray-blonde hair curls around her face, framing features that are currently pinched in curiosity. "Can I help you?"

I'm grateful that her tone is more puzzled than unkind because while I've given myself mental pep talks for what I'm going to say to Penn, introducing myself to his family was not what I imagined.

Not that I mind, of course.

He put up with meeting my parents and all my siblings in one go, so the least I can do is exchange pleasantries with the woman who raised him.

"Hi," I say, renewing my grasp on my bag.

She lets out a laugh on a breath. "Hello."

"Is Penn home by any chance?"

"He is." She pauses as she assesses my nervous fidgeting. "And who are you?"

"I'm a…friend of his," I manage. "I'm Violet."

"Oh," she says, immediately brightening at my name. "Of course you are. Please, come in."

I step over the threshold and note the very organized pile of shoes by the door, then cringe at the memory of how many people didn't abide by that courtesy at the house party.

"I'm Mary," she tells me as she shuts the front door.

"It's nice to meet you," I say genuinely, although I wish I had more to add.

Mary smiles approvingly at my politeness. "Likewise."

As I slip out of my tennis shoes, I glance around, finding that her presence and a few candles have warmed the place in a way that feels even more homey than the last time I was here.

"Penn's up in his room," she says, gesturing up the stairs.

I nod as I start up that way. "Great."

"It's at the end of the hall on the left," she adds.

I hesitate on the second step, recalling she's unaware of the social gathering or my presence here before.

"Thank you," I say graciously before bounding up the remaining stairs.

There are a few pictures on the walls that I missed the first time around, and while some of them are pure entertainment—like a young Penn wearing Mickey Mouse ears—the others make my heart ache.

For the majority of Penn's younger life, his parents appear as fixtures by his side. There's even one of the three of them in which he's all decked out in hockey gear. And then, as he grows older, they just...stop appearing.

But in *all* the pictures, Penn maintains his classic smile.

As I step toward his door, I take a breath to collect myself, then knock.

Unlike Mary's slow approach, Penn answers immediately. "Come in," he calls.

I open the door and take in the sight of Penn's hunched-over posture.

He sits on the edge of his bed with his fingers twitching over a bright green N64 controller.

"Hang on, Nana," he says, gaze fixed on the screen. "I'm about to beat this boss. Agh!"

Penn grits his teeth as his pixelated character moves around the arena. It appears he's trying to kill two flying witches. The music is frantic, heightening the anxiety I feel while watching him try not to fall off the ledge of some high platform.

"No, no, no," he whines as he gets hit again.

The remaining heart gets grayed out, which apparently means he's dead, then his character is dropped back at the entrance of whatever building he was just in.

Penn lets out a loud sigh as he saves the game and moves to flip the system off. "What did you—"

He stops speaking when he turns and sees me leaning against his doorframe.

An amused smile overtakes my features. "Hi."

He blinks rapidly. "Hi."

"What game was that?" I ask.

Originally, I had planned to start with an apology for not getting in touch sooner, but I'm happy to have a much less intense icebreaker.

"*Ocarina of Time*," he says like it's obvious. "The best Zelda game ever in my opinion. Some say it might even be the best game ever made."

I slowly step into his room, then sit on the edge of his bed. "Oh, really?"

"Yeah. I mean, nostalgia aside, the mechanics of game-play and the world-building and the level of detail—" He shakes his head. "Sorry, I'm rambling. What are you doing here?"

He's looking at me slightly wide-eyed.

It sets off my own panic until he runs his fingers through his hair, tucking a few strands behind his ears— and I realize I've caught him completely off guard.

I've never done that before.

And I like how powerful it makes me feel.

"Is it not okay that I came over?" I clarify.

"Of course it's okay," he says quickly. "I'm just surprised because I haven't heard from you. I actually wondered…uh…"

"You wondered?" I prompt.

Penn runs his teeth over his bottom lip as he considers how to phrase his thoughts. "If I overdid it or something?"

I shake my head. "No. Definitely not. I had a great time on Saturday."

He lets out a breath of relief, and I can see the tension in his shoulders dissipate as he sits beside me, buckling his mattress enough that I have to press my weight into my feet so I don't slide into him.

"I talked to Charlie the next day, and he told me it was really weird that I, like, invited myself into your plans," Penn explains. "He made it seem like I might have over- stayed my welcome or something. And when I didn't hear from you, I just assumed he was right."

"He was very wrong," I assure him. "And if you're up for it, I'm ready for our second date."

His eyes flash in excitement as I hand over the bag I brought.

"What's this?" he asks.

I chuckle. "Open it and find out."

He does as I suggest, but his look of confusion remains in place as he pulls out the contents. "A bowl, and a brush, and…" He glances up after reading the label on the bottle. "Hair dye."

"Only if you're still up for it," I say quickly.

He jumps up. "Oh, hell yes."

His enthusiasm is infectious as he leads me back into the hall and over to the bathroom.

"Does this work?" Penn asks, gesturing to the space as he flips on the light.

It's a simple setup of a vanity, toilet, and bathtub-shower combo. Although it doesn't have the step stool that I usually make June sit on or the old robes we wear to protect our clothes, it'll do just fine.

"It does," I answer. "Have a seat."

He sits on the lid of the toilet without an ounce of embarrassment, then watches patiently as I get organized on the counter.

I set out all the materials, including my gloves and a plastic shower cap, then reach for the black hairbrush that's poking out of the drawer.

"Do you mind?" I ask, holding it up by the handle.

"I don't," he says.

I step forward, but the gravity of my innocent intention doesn't hit me until I run my fingers through his hair, and his body relaxes as he leans into my touch.

I'm an idiot for not realizing how intimate this experience would be. It's probably because I'm used to having to scold June to hold still or set up a complex system of mirrors to coat the back of my own hair.

"This is nice already," Penn whispers.

I hum in response, then continue.

I take my time working through his hair, gently brushing out two tricky knots before it's ready to start sectioning.

"I was worried I was going to have to bleach your hair, since it's a little darker," I murmur as I trade the brush for a pair of gloves. "But I think it'll be fine to just go for it. The color won't be as vibrant as June's, but you'll be able to see it for sure."

Penn has a sleepy and content look on his face. "Whatever you think is best."

"A lot of trust here," I joke.

He nods. "Definitely."

My setup isn't professional by any means, but I've done this enough times that I have a bit of a routine.

I've learned from my mistakes, so I take my time mixing the color and conditioner, as recommended by the manufacturer—and all the videos I watched on YouTube—before I officially start.

Penn is quiet, patient, and almost contemplative as I work to ensure each section of hair is coated properly before moving on to the next.

It takes me about forty minutes to do the job, then I drag my fingers through his hair, double-checking my work before I take off my gloves.

"You know, I think we're doing this whole thing right," Penn says.

I sit on the edge of the tub, admiring him and my handiwork. "Yeah?"

"Grocery shopping, dinner, dessert, and what did June

call it? 'Sister spa party.'"

I let out a snort. "If this is a sister spa party, we're missing some things."

"Like what?" Penn asks.

I tick the items off on my fingers. "Nail painting, face masks, occasional makeup application, maybe some dress-up, and, oh, an overbearing June. She is a key part of it."

"Maybe next time," he says with a grin.

"I do like that we are doing things non-traditionally." I pause and wring my hands. "Not that I'm sure what exactly is traditional."

Penn quirks a brow. "Oh yeah?"

"Yeah," I say.

"Well, I can definitely say this is a first for me," he says after a beat. "How long do I have to let it set?"

"Twenty minutes or so."

He settles back, getting more comfortable. "Okay."

"Make sure you don't get any dye on the wall," I warn. "It'll never come out."

"I'm watching," he assures me.

As he adjusts his stance, our knees knock together—at first by accident, and then he does it deliberately, earning himself a smile.

"For the record, Violet," Penn says, voice low and as intense as I've ever heard it. "I barely know you, and I already feel like it could be really real, you know? Like we're on the edge, and if we both went all-in, it could really be something."

I have to pretend that those words don't rock my entire world.

Because not only is it kind of out of nowhere but it's intense, just like he is.

I decide I like the declaration, but I can't form any sort of coherent thought or sentence after that, so I merely press my lips together and nod.

"How's that for bucking tradition?" Penn teases.

"Pretty good."

"I bet you don't get any sort of thoughts like that at your sister spa parties."

"No, definitely not."

"Good," he says confidently. "But as far as the norm goes, now that we've met each other's family, I think we're checking off the list pretty nicely."

"As long as it's not written out like your grocery lists," I retort.

He playfully huffs at that.

"But, uh," I falter, trying to decide how to word my next sentence. "I met Mary. Obviously. She seems nice."

"She's the best," he says promptly. "Comes to all my games. Makes the best ziti. Is there whenever I need her. Goes away for a weekend so I can throw a rager."

I chuckle as I shake my head. "Everything a person could ask for in a grandparent, really."

"But I am a little nervous for next year," he tells me seriously, lifting a hand to run it through his hair, only to stop halfway when he recalls he can't.

"What about it?" I ask.

"I worry about her being alone in the house when I'm off at school. She wants me to go wherever I want, but I hate the idea of being so far away for that long."

"That's sweet of you to worry."

"It's just reality." Penn shrugs. "She had a bad fall a couple of years ago. I actually had to stay with Charlie's family while she was in the hospital. She made a full recovery, but I don't think I'll ever forget coming home from school to see her sprawled out on the floor and crying in pain."

I frown at the visual, understanding how that would have distressed him. "You don't think about staying closer to home, then? Going to one of the schools in the city?"

"Oh, all the time, but she won't hear it," Penn admits with a laugh. "In fact, if she had her way, she'd ship me off to live in Greenland or somewhere just as cold so I could play outside all year long."

"She's a big fan, then?"

"Understatement," Penn tells me, then his eyes flash. "Hey, are you coming to the game tomorrow?"

I tap my fingers against the edge of the tub. "I was planning on it."

"Well, Nana's going, too. If you need some company in the stands, maybe you could join her?"

"My, uh, friends from my school will be there, too."

"Right." Penn nods at that realization. "You going to be torn on who to root for, then?"

"No way," I say immediately. "Whatever team Kara is on has my loyalty."

"Wow," he scoffs, acting like he's affronted. "That hurts."

"I think you'll recover." I roll my eyes. "And it's probably time to wash the dye out."

"Okay."

He stands up, but as he eyes the spigot, then me, it's

immediately clear he's not sure of the logistics.

"I can step out so you can shower," I offer, then eye his height against the edge of the tub. "Or if you sit right here and lean back, I can wash it out for you."

Penn's eyes dart toward the floor, then he nods. "If you don't mind."

"Well, it's hardly the sister spa party experience if you don't get fully pampered," I reply lightly.

He chuckles before he gets in position, leaning forward when I tell him to so I can put a towel behind his neck, tucking it so the edges don't bite into his skin.

Thankfully, this setup has one of those fancy detachable showerheads, so once the water hits the right temperature, I take it down and start rinsing out the color.

I should have left my gloves on for this because the purple dye is heavy, but I let the water pressure do most of the work before I start rubbing his scalp with my fingertips.

He closes his eyes as I move, and although my heart pounds at our proximity, there's no denying it's awkward to shampoo him from this angle.

My arms burn as I hold them up, which is as uncomfortable as it is embarrassing to learn how out of shape I am.

I push through until my upper back starts to stiffen, then I pause my ministrations to crack my neck in an attempt to relieve the tension.

"You okay?" Penn asks, opening one eye.

I nod as I shake out my shoulders. "I'm almost done."

"Here," he offers.

I don't know what he's doing until his hands come to my hips to guide me.

The force of his movement causes me to jerk awkwardly, but he encourages me to move so my knees are on the outsides of his thighs.

I force myself not to look at him—knowing that doing so will cause me to melt into a puddle of red-faced embarrassment—and ignore the fact that I am *straddling* him while shampooing his hair.

After a few minutes, the water runs completely clear, and I condition the ends of his hair before giving him a final rinse.

As I lean over to turn off the faucet, I catch Penn's expression.

His eyes are closed, but his hands are still lightly gripping my waist, holding me to him.

With both amusement and awe, I note his complete trust in my actions. I mean, I could have fried his hair or ruined it, but he's at peace with whatever the result may be.

"All done," I murmur as I hang the showerhead on the hook, then reach back for a towel.

He swallows as he glances up at me, and I watch the movement in his throat, barely stopping myself from running my fingertips over it.

My self-control propels me to stand up, forcing Penn to drop his hold, take the towel when I offer it, and run it through his hair.

I step back, giving him some space.

"This is awesome," Penn says as he steps closer to the mirror to admire my work.

I can't help but smile at his appraisal.

Because I agree.

As promised, the shade isn't as vibrant a violet as it could be, but it *works* for him, and he wears it with the confidence of some sort of grungy rockstar.

"I'm glad you like it," I tell him.

He shakes his head. "I *love* it. Thank you."

"You're welcome. And thank you right back."

"For what?" he asks with a smile.

"The second date," I answer. "And…for being you."

He smirks, then runs the towel through his hair again, drying it as best he can. "You hungry?"

"I could eat."

"Good," he says, holding out his hand.

I don't hesitate to take it.

And I'm reminded that our fingers fit perfectly together —and that it feels natural to hold onto each other as we walk, even though he takes the stairs a little bit faster than I do.

He drops my grasp to slide open the pocket door to the kitchen, revealing Mary sitting at the table, eating a leftover piece of pumpkin pie.

She glances up at us with a smile, then her eyes widen in surprise. "What on earth!"

Penn makes a big show of twirling around so she can see his new hair from every angle. "Violet did it for me."

"I guessed as much," she says.

He drops a kiss on her cheek, then steps to the fridge and starts pulling out various dishes and containers.

"What do you think?" Penn asks her as he moves.

Mary takes in his bouncy movements and his casual smile as he prepares our lunch, then she looks at me once more. "I think Violet is my new favorite color."

FIFTEEN

"Alex is playing *great*," Erica says, voice dripping with admiration.

It's probably the tenth time she's said something along those lines since the game started, and I, once again, pick up on a hint of nerves and trepidation in her words, which I don't exactly understand.

Because her eyes have remained mostly on Kara.

I don't call her out on it because I'm already on thin ice —pun intended.

I earned a glare of disapproval when I joined her in the stands wearing one of Kara's spare jerseys, wanting to show my support, even though I doubt she can see me among all the fans.

In turn, Erica is all decked out in her own way—she painted Alex's number on her face and tied some red tinsel into her hair to show her team spirit.

"This is really violent," Emily crows with glee as two players are slammed up against the plexiglass wall.

"Well," Erica starts with an air of importance. "Alex says that hockey requires an incredible level of skill compared to any other sport. I mean, it ties the physicality of MMA with the precision of golf and the movement of running, like basketball and soccer do, but it's even more challenging because they're on skates."

"Makes sense," I agree, having heard a similar line of thinking from Kara many times.

Emily frowns. "Such a shame it's hidden under all that padding."

Erica laughs. "Without it, the game would be even more dangerous. Alex says that…"

I tune her out, unable to handle another round of "Alex says," and try to focus on the game.

It's honestly easy to do because while I feel nervous watching Kara, I'm exhilarated when Penn takes off down the ice.

Despite Emily's claim, I can envision the lines of muscle and bulk underneath the players' uniforms, but it also helps that I've seen the way Penn's shirts cling to his body.

Somehow, I find him just as alluring now as he glides effortlessly on his skates while one of his teammates stick-handles.

There's a sudden flash of movement.

And everything happens so fast that I almost miss it, but my eyes adjust right as Penn shoots, then the puck hits the back of the net.

I silently cheer as his whole team celebrates.

"Damn," Erica's voice rings out among the collective disappointment of our classmates.

It's been interesting to experience the game among the section of yelling fans that are our classmates, but it's taken me two full periods to realize that I much prefer to sit and watch these on my own, in silence.

And although I don't expect the entire arena to be mute, I could do without Erica's commentary.

"I'm going to go get a drink," I announce to no one in particular.

I mutter a dozen apologies as I sidestep through the row and into the aisle, then I make my way to the concession stand.

Marshall's arena is a little bit nicer than Greene's, so I have more than one food and drink option, but I simply go for the shortest line, not wanting to miss too much of the action.

I buy a hot chocolate and a pretzel for good measure, using the comfort of carbohydrates to soothe myself in the presence of my "friends."

As I make my way back to my seat, a warm voice calls out for me.

"Violet!"

I turn to see Mary's very bundled form a few rows up.

She's wearing a puffy winter coat that looks more like a sleeping bag than a jacket, and her knit hat is complete with fur-lined earflaps that frame her face.

I can't help but break out into a smile when she waves enthusiastically for me to join her.

"Hi, Mary," I say in greeting as I bounce up the steps.

"Don't just stand there," she says with a laugh, batting my shoulder. "Join us, will you?"

"Happy to."

I take the seat beside her, and as soon as I'm settled, she pulls some of her blanket over my knees.

The gesture warms me—and not just temperature-wise.

"I swear these games get colder every year," she says with a huff.

"You're just getting older, Mary," a similarly aged man teases.

"Oh, quiet, you," she shushes him.

"It's fine," he says, leaning across her to speak to me. "She knows I like older women."

Mary lets out an exaggerated sigh.

I quirk an eyebrow before I take a massive bite of salty pretzel.

"This is Jeff," Mary explains quickly. "He's with me."

I nod as I swallow. "Hi. I'm Violet."

"A pleasure to meet you, Violet," Jeff says in a very charming, deep voice.

I smile at him, taking in his silver-gray hair and well-kept beard. His name definitely fits him—he gives off a kind of Jeff Bridges vibe, and Mary, despite feigning annoy-ance, looks totally smitten.

"He is *two years* younger than me," she grumbles.

Jeff chuckles and pulls off her mitten so he can kiss the back of her hand.

I tilt my head and assess them. "Are you two—"

"Boyfriend and girlfriend? Dating? Going steady?" Jeff grins. "Yep. All of it. You see, it all started when—"

"That's enough," Mary says, patting his thigh.

"Oh, come on," he retorts. "I'm just getting to know Penn's *friend*."

I don't know what his emphasis means, but I'm too shy to ask for clarification.

Mary glares at him. "I'm here to watch my grandson, not listen to you yammer on about how we got set up by our friends."

"Are you sure you don't want to hear how I thought, no, I *knew*, you'd be the most beautiful woman in any room?" He smiles as he nudges her. "And that red dress you were wearing…I still have dreams about that, you know."

"Jeff," she warns.

"All right, all right," he relents.

I smile as I turn my attention back to the game.

Their dynamic and banter is much, *much* more enjoyable than Erica's endless droning, but I don't get to hear much of it because the last period of the game is intense—especially after one of Alex's teammates scores and brings it to a tie in the last two minutes.

I know some of the statistics and plays just from passing curiosity and being Kara's best friend for so long, but I try to pull back from all that. I try to simply watch like everyone else as the time ticks down and Kara makes an incredible save off her blocker, sending the puck a few feet back on the ice.

I whoop and yell, applauding for my best friend as the other players scramble to take control.

In the bustle of activity, Alex breaks away with the puck, and one of Greene's defenders practically tackles him to the ground.

The move earns Alex a penalty shot.

Gripping my now-empty hot chocolate cup, I scoot to

the edge of my seat, unable to look away as he skates around his own goal almost carelessly.

Then Alex takes off, moving down the ice and batting the puck as he goes.

The other players and referees are off to the side, giving him a clear path to Greene's goal, so it's just Kara standing in his way.

She hunches into position, shifting her legs and adjusting the grip on her stick as she tries to predict his next play.

Both Alex and the puck move too fast for me to see, but he takes his shot—

And it's impossible to miss the triumphant sound Alex cries out.

Or the way his teammates dash in his direction and pummel him in celebration.

The entire home spectator section, where I started the game, erupts into cheers, but Mary, Jeff, and those around me let out an almost collective sigh.

The action on the ice resumes, very briefly and with a pointed energy shift, until the final buzzer sounds.

"Well, that's that, I suppose," Mary says.

"Can't win them all," Jeff adds.

I nod as I stand to help her fold up her blanket, then toss out my trash as we make our way to the lobby.

I glance back once, expecting to see the teams lining up on the ice for their post-game handshake, but they're already making their way to their respective locker rooms.

"Not the result we wanted," Jeff says as he takes the bundle of belongings from Mary's hands. "But a good game nonetheless."

"I just know that Kara is going to be really upset," I say.

Mary shrugs. "When it comes to penalty shots, it's almost luck whether you're able to stop it. Really, the blame should be on the player who fouled, not the person who has to defend a net against a puck that's flying toward them at ninety miles per hour."

I manage a smile. "I'll pass that along."

"Are you going to stick around for a bit?" Mary asks. "Wait for Penn to—"

"Violet!"

It's Emily's voice, but when I turn to face her, my eyes land on a scowling Erica.

"Where have you *been?*" Erica demands.

"I got…sidetracked," I say, nodding to Mary and Jeff.

Erica forces her mouth into a flat line before she answers, apparently not wanting to be outright rude in front of adults. "Well, we're having a victory party at Alex's tonight. I'll drive you over if you want."

"You're coming, right?" Emily presses.

"I'm actually going to pass," I say. "I'll hang around here for a bit."

Erica rolls her eyes and turns away. "Picking Kara, of course."

"Excuse me?" I snap, stepping forward.

She comes to a halt and whips around because the harshness of my tone apparently shocks her just as much as it does me.

"I just…" She lets out a sigh. "We're here to support *my* boyfriend, and you show up wearing the other team's jersey? It's pretty disrespectful."

I lift my eyebrows high in surprise and irritation. "I'm

not here to support *your* boyfriend. I'm here to support *my* best friend."

I have the awareness to be embarrassed that this conversation is happening right in front of Mary and Jeff, but a quick glance in their direction reveals amused smiles.

"Whatever," Erica says. "Have fun with that."

She loops her arm through Emily's, and they stomp off, their steps in sync.

"What nice girls." Mary breaks the silence, tone light as I continue to stare at their backs. "Friends of yours?"

I frown as they push through the exit. "Used to be."

SIXTEEN

I manage to avoid my school's team by hiding in the little arcade section of the lobby.

I scan all the retro games, wondering if Penn loves pinball as much as he does the modern consoles in his room. Given that he has pretty much every system I've ever heard of—and more—I wouldn't be surprised if his interest bleeds over into the broader genre.

There are a few kids wasting their dollars on the claw machine. They're attempting to pull out a couple of stuffed dinosaurs that are definitely cheaper to buy than what the kids are spending by trying to win them.

But I guess their parents are just grateful that they're entertained for a few minutes.

Which I can definitely understand.

I once endured listening to that obnoxious shark song for an entire hour to keep The Baby occupied while I did my chemistry homework.

"Violet," Penn calls.

I glance up and am momentarily dumbfounded by his appearance—his purple hair in disarray, smelling of his eucalyptus shampoo, and a wide grin on his face.

"Kara already left," he informs me. "That is, if you're waiting around for her and not me."

"Both," I say with a smile. "But, really? She's gone?"

His features pull into a frown. "She's pretty bummed about the game. It's not her fault, of course. The penalty was on Daniel. But that other goal…I mean, our defense left her wide open."

I like that even after a loss, he's still level-headed and a staunch defender of Kara.

"She said she wanted to go home and 'eat her feelings,'" Penn tells me. "Which are her words, not mine, along with her plan to watch 'all the bad television in the world.'"

"It's her comfort move," I say knowingly as I pull out my phone to text her.

I heard you left, but I wanted to say that you played great. Let me know if you need me to come over bearing gifts (baked goods and Doritos).

It doesn't take long for her response to come through. *I just want to be alone tonight.*

Okay. But seriously. Let me know.

Will do.

Love you.

Love you, too. Go out with Penn tonight, but bring me desserts tomorrow. Please.

I laugh as I hold up my phone for him to read.

"Well, if Kara insists…"

"You don't have to hang with the team tonight?" I ask

curiously. "No smiley cookies or giving pep talks or analyzing mistakes or something?"

He shakes his head. "Coach went pretty hard on us after the game, so I think everyone needs a day to cool off."

"Seems wise."

"Practice is probably going to be brutal next week, though, since we're already starting to eye postseason stuff. If all goes according to plan, we shouldn't actually have to travel too far on the road, which means Nana won't have to drive as long at night."

"Oh, that reminds me," I say quickly. "I wanted to tell you. I took you up on your suggestion to sit with Mary. She and her...uh, Jeff, already took off, though."

"Well, then," Penn holds out his hand. "Looks like it's just you and me. Date number three?"

I lace my fingers through his as we walk. "Already? Feels like date number two was just yesterday."

He smirks. "And to think you were worried we'd run out of things to talk about."

"Look at us go."

He opens the door to his truck, helping me step up into it before he walks around and dumps his bag in the back.

"What do we do now?" I ask as he slides into the driver's seat.

"I've got a few ideas," he says brightly before turning the key in the ignition.

I quirk a brow. "Like what?"

"Well, I was thinking we could start with doing something one of us likes and see if the other person enjoys it, too. And we can trade off from there."

I consider that and find no flaw in his logic. "Sounds reasonable. Do you want first pick?"

Penn shakes his head. "But I do want to know…if we weren't hanging out tonight, what would you be doing instead?"

"Hanging with June or Kara, doing homework, baking, the usual stuff." I cringe at how lame all my options sound.

He laughs. "Well, we've done those things already. And I definitely enjoyed them. But let's say you wanted a break from all that. Like, if you were ravenous after an hour and a half of skating on ice. Where would you go?"

"Are you hungry?" I ask in amusement.

"I'm always hungry," he says. "And while I don't think all of our activities have to be food-based, I could *really* go for something good right now."

I snicker. "I should have expected it, knowing Kara's bottomless appetite after playing."

"It comes with the territory."

"Right," I say as I try to think of a good place for us to go.

Everything I run through my mind feels too formal or too kid-friendly, and I'm not in the mood for either. I just want to enjoy the night with Penn and perhaps indulge my sweet tooth without having to put in all the effort myself.

"The coffeeshop where my mom works has really good cookies," I say casually. "And it's open late tonight."

"Lead the way."

And I'm happy to discover that, since I'm not hunched over a notepad and stressed about the bake sale for this visit, I actually get to enjoy the ride.

It's almost stupid how much fun I have scrolling

through his playlists and picking out songs I like, too. We also talk about the different tracks and the trivia behind some of the lyrics, and our back and forth continues easily as I direct him toward Books & Beans.

By the time we step up to the counter, I feel comfortable enough to take the initiative and touch him, placing my hand on his arm as I point out some of my favorite items.

The light contact doesn't go unnoticed, and he smiles as he scans the available options.

"Hey, Violet," Marie says as she steps out from the back of the shop. "I didn't know you'd be in tonight."

"We're feeling hungry, and you've got the best grilled cheese in town," I say simply before I turn to Penn. "This is Marie, my mom's boss and the owner."

Marie's gaze flicks up to his hair, then she smiles. "You must be Penn."

It's no surprise to discover my mother has been gossiping about me at work.

"I am," he says immediately. "It's nice to meet you."

"He's my...boyfriend," I announce, testing out the word.

It's not something we've discussed, but I think it's inevitable that we're crawling toward those monikers.

My boldness earns the biggest grin yet from Penn.

"Well, I'm glad you're both here," Marie says kindly. "What can I get for you?"

I glance sideways at Penn, and he waves me on in encouragement.

"Can I get a grilled cheese?" I ask politely. "And one of the white chocolate red velvet cookies, please?"

"Of course," Marie says, then she eyes Penn.

"I've got it," he says quickly, stepping forward and pulling out his wallet.

She gives me a wink before she returns her focus wholly to him.

"Can we also get another grilled cheese," Penn says. "And the club sandwich. And, is that a veggie BLT?"

She laughs at his enthusiasm. "Yep."

"One of those, too, please. And what's this cookie right here? Chocolate peanut butter with Reese's Pieces? Actually, you know what?" His eyes wander over the entire display case. "Can we just get one of each of these cookies?"

"Of course. You'll even get a discount on a half dozen."

"Perfect," he says, then glances at me. "Anything else?"

"I'm good," I tell them both. "Thank you."

Penn swipes his card, but judging by the total, Marie has given us a very generous discount, which he all but cancels out with a massive tip.

"I'll bring everything out in a few minutes," Marie says before addressing the customer behind us.

We step out of the way so she can carry on her business.

"Thank you, Penn," I say.

He inclines his head. "I am happy to treat my *girlfriend*."

I actually giggle at that.

He beams before he surveys the nearly empty space. "What table do you like?"

"Any of them," I say nonchalantly as I move toward the first available seat.

He steps forward, directly in my way. "Definitely not that one."

I balk. "What? What's wrong with it?"

"It's all about the ambiance, you see," he tells me.

I do see, which is exactly why I chose this place, but he seems to be even more picky than me.

"This table is too close to the counter," he insists. "I mean, we could be having a very private and personal conversation and be interrupted or distracted by all the other people waiting."

"Okay, I'll give you that." I point out another random seat. "What about that one?"

"A little too close to the entrance. And your jacket doesn't look all that warm."

"It's warm enough," I protest. "I did just sit through an entire hockey game in it."

"Yeah, but Nana gave you most of her blanket."

My jaw drops open. "You were scoping me out in the stands?"

Penn lets out a laugh. "Of course. What, you think all my trick moves were just to show off? I was trying to impress you."

"Oh really?"

"Really," he says easily, then leads us over to another spot.

"Is this the one?"

He nods. "This is us."

It's a wooden table set for four people, just like all the others, but it's strategically placed by the window and gives us a good vantage point for the entire store.

"Any preference on seating?" I ask before I claim a chair for myself.

He forces a look of horror. "You're not one of those same-side sitters, are you?"

"Oh, absolutely not," I assure him as I sink down. "I'm not a psychopath. The only appropriate time for that is sitting on barstools in my opinion."

He takes the chair directly across from me, playfully knocking our knees together. "Good. This could have all been ruined."

"Three dates, and you'd kick me to the curb over that?" I say, aghast.

"Definitely. I can tolerate a questionable song choice here and there, but given that I plan to eat a lot of meals with you, this could frame the entire crux of our relationship."

I like hearing him use that term to describe what we're doing.

"Here you are," Marie announces.

She slides a tray, which is almost overflowing, onto the end of our table, then smiles at me before she makes herself scarce.

"So, maybe we should get all those things out of the way, then?" Penn suggests as he tugs the tray over, settling it between us.

"What things?" I ask, reaching for my grilled cheese.

I know the perfectly toasted bread and savory, melty cheddar will be delicious, but the gooey strands are a little difficult to navigate with any semblance of table manners.

Penn seems unfazed by my struggle, though, and takes a bite of his own.

"Oh my god, that's good as hell," he says before

pressing a napkin to his lips. "But I mean that we should work out all the 'hard nos.'"

"Okay," I agree. "What are some of yours?"

"Well, aside from the usual things like not wanting to spend time with someone who robs banks or something—"

"Stealing money and sitting on the same side of a table are equally inexcusable."

Penn holds his arms up like he's a ringmaster at a circus. "You get me."

I shake my head as I laugh and take another bite.

"Anyway, let's see," he says, refocusing on me. "I can't stand when people whistle."

"At all? Or just out of tune?"

"Anytime," he says seriously, digging into the first of his cookies. "I don't know why, but there's just something about it that makes my skin crawl."

"Is it because you can't do it?" I challenge.

He gives his best attempt at a glare. "No."

"Fine. But while we're on this line of thinking, I should tell you that I can't stand the smacking sound of people chewing gum."

"I get that. But what about blowing bubbles? Does the popping sound bug you?"

"No, just the sound of the rubbery material between people's molars." I shiver, repulsed at the thought. "I can't stand it."

"What about handholding in public?" Penn asks jovially, reaching over to squeeze my hand once before he picks up the other half of his BLT.

I know he's trying to be playful, but the question stops me short.

It's not that I'm averse to doing so, but every single time I see Alex and Erica making public displays of affection, my entire body gets irritated, starting with a discomfort in my chest.

I don't know if it's just my reaction to them or if it's people in general, though, so I'll need to test my theory.

"I think I'm okay with it," I hedge as I reach for my dessert. "As long as the gesture isn't holding up traffic or making anyone else uncomfortable."

"Does anything make *you* uncomfortable?" Penn asks, tone serious as much as it is curious.

"Not that I know of," I say. "It's just…Erica and her boyfriend are always excessively touching each other, and it drives me insane."

"Why's that?"

"It's not…jealousy or anything." I pause to consider my next words. "I don't really like the guy that much, so every touch they share is just a reminder that he's in my life and hers, and it's grating."

He nods sympathetically. "I get it."

I let out a breath before I speak. "Actually, you know him."

"What?"

"Erica's dating that guy Alex Turner. He plays for my school."

The deep groan Penn lets out startles me.

He presses his lips together. "I'm sorry, but I really can't stand that guy. He might as well be at the top of my 'hard no' list."

"Do you know him well?"

"We both tried out for a travel team a few years ago,

and we've been bumping into each other ever since." Penn shakes his head at whatever memory is surfacing in his mind. "Let's just say that he doesn't exactly get along with my friends, and the feeling is mutual."

I nod. "My entire life, I've been best friends with Kara and Erica, but lately, with the latter, it feels like things aren't the same. And I think Alex and my *deep* dislike for him has a lot to do with it. It's definitely not the only thing, but still, I just...can't believe that our friendship has changed simply because she got a boyfriend."

"Well, now that you have a *boyfriend*, do you think things will be different?"

I take a bite of a cookie to give myself a second. "I'm hoping that you and I can still be the same people, just together."

He grins at my words. "I like that. But I should tell you that I once heard someone say we're the summation of the five people we spend the most time with."

"Oh, god," I groan. "Please don't tell me that my siblings are helping to shape my personality."

"I don't think that would be a bad thing."

"Considering they're all whistling, gum-chewing, sticky monsters, you might be changing your mind soon," I warn him.

"I'll try to work through it," he tells me seriously. "Because I'm starting to think that you and I could do anything."

His words are brave and maybe a little premature, but I appreciate it.

"I hope so," I say quietly.

Penn wipes his hands on his napkin before he leans

back in his chair. "See how many things seemed so heavy until we've released them into the air? We've really paved the way for success here, getting this all out there now."

"I like the way you think."

"Well, I like *you*, Violet."

"Same."

He chuckles as he slings his arm around the vacant seat beside him. "You like yourself or you like me?"

I take a slow bite, just to make him wait. "Both."

"Good." Penn suddenly leans forward, gripping the edge of the table. "There's one other thing, though."

"Okay?" I say skeptically.

And before I even know what's happening, he leans forward and presses his lips against mine.

Our first kiss happens right here at our perfectly selected table that's covered in cookie crumbs.

It's immediately so warm, wonderful, and tingle-inducing that I can't fathom doing anything other than kissing him back.

He tastes of sugar, and the movement is sweet, but it's over almost as quickly as it started.

I open my eyes to see his face flushed and smile some-what reserved.

"Well?" Penn prompts, waiting for my review.

"I like that," I tell him hoarsely.

"See?" He's immensely smug and proud—I can tell as much in his demeanor and words. "I knew we'd find things in common."

SEVENTEEN

"Mom, I'm home," I call up the stairs.

It's a needless declaration, given that she likely heard the garage door, but I announce myself anyway.

I think it's because I'm feeling overly excited and agreeable, which has been my state of mind since Penn kissed me yesterday.

It also helps that I've spent the last four hours at Kara's rehashing every single detail while scarfing down the nachos and s'mores we made in the microwave.

She's already gotten over the loss from yesterday because the flood of supportive messages from her teammates in the group text—led by Penn—helped soothe her sadness.

And although I tried to tell her what Mary said—that in those shootout situations, it's up to fate more than her skill—she seemed more interested in hearing me talk about Penn and our growing feelings for each other.

She pressed for every single detail, including exactly

how I felt while he was kissing me and how *sensual* it was that I, essentially, helped him take a shower.

I don't exactly see it that way, but I understand what she means.

Penn and I have a level of intimacy now, and the mere prospect of its existence scared me at first, but I actually find it easy...and comforting...and delightful.

All of which contributes to my general elation, even as I do something as mundane as kick off my tennis shoes and arrange them on the rack.

"Mom?" I call out, wondering where everyone is.

I'm distracted by Penn's incoming text—a picture of a cool cloud formation he just saw at the start of his eight-mile run.

He now knows that while some people prefer stargazing, I'm definitely more about staring up at the little white fluffballs during the day.

It was one of the thousand things we talked about last night while grazing on the remainder of our food at Books & Beans—my love of science, his earliest memories of hockey, the time Chloe accidentally shut the car door on my pinky finger and broke it, the day Nana attempted to teach Penn how to shave his face, and so many other little things I now know about him that only serve to endear him more to me.

In short, I feel happy—blissful, even.

And I'm enjoying every second of it.

"Can you come in here, Violet?" Ryan calls from his office.

I'm still so in my own head that I don't register his tone

is off, but as I turn down the hallway, his words and forced lightness roll in like a shadow.

"Are you okay?" I ask as I push open the door to Ryan's office, nearly hitting him with it.

My gaze immediately lands on my mother, who sits primly at my stepdad's desk, and her expression is a little guarded.

"Everything's just fine," she says immediately, though I don't buy it.

"Violet..." Ryan's mouth forms into a flat line.

A looming presence in my periphery makes me turn, and I gasp at the sight of my biological father leaning casually against a set of bookshelves.

I openly gape at him, unable to process that he's really here.

"There she is," he says cheerfully. "We've been waiting for your arrival."

I turn back to Ryan, unsure of what to say or do, but his expression doesn't change—he simply waits for me to react.

My father opens his arms for a hug. "It's so good to see you."

I take a pointed step back, making it clear that I'm not interested in his embrace, and he claps his hands together instead.

"What's going on?" I direct the question to my mother, whose mouth is now turned down in a frown.

"I came to see you, Violet," my father explains. "It's been too long."

"Has it?" I ask coolly.

He chuckles. "Of course. I've missed you every single day since we last spoke."

I narrow my eyes at him. "That's nice."

"Violet," my mom says with a slight warning to her tone.

It's not that she's on my dad's side—she's simply a peacekeeper.

And I suppose she sees my rudeness as a direct reflection of her parenting because she's raised me better than to disrespect anyone so blatantly—no matter how badly I want to.

"Is there something you need from me?"

My father maintains his charming disposition, but I can see a tightness forming around his eyes.

It's the only crack in his well-crafted facade.

"I was hoping we could talk, actually," he says lightly.

"Sure." I cross my arms over my chest. "Go ahead."

He looks at my mom and Ryan, quirking a brow in silent question.

"Your father has some news to share," my mother says.

"And I was hoping to talk to you one on one," he adds.

"But only if that's okay with you, Violet," Ryan says quickly.

I sink my teeth into my lip, wanting to explode and shout that in *no way* is this okay, but I trust him and my mom to not put me in any situation where I might feel uncomfortable or unsafe.

Although I'm not thrilled with my father's surprise visit, I don't think he's a threat, and I am curious enough to hear him out.

"It's okay," I say eventually.

"Good," Ryan says, expressing his approval with that one word. "We'll be in the kitchen if you need us."

"Well, what's left of it, anyway," my mom mutters. "We left June in charge."

That remark, along with Ryan's small smile and encouraging nod, is enough to ease some of the tension I'm carrying in my body.

I take my mother's spot, sitting in the comfortable leather office chair, then I lace my fingers together on Ryan's desk like I'm the president waiting for my chief of staff to give me an update.

My father clears his throat as he takes the seat opposite me.

I like that his chair is a few inches lower than mine, making up the difference in our heights so that we're eye to eye.

"So, Violet, how have you been?"

"Fine."

I give him the one-word answer just to be petulant, then revel in the awkward silence that settles between us.

"That's…good. Your hair is different." He scans me like he's trying to pull out anything else he can comment on to make this conversation go smoother. "I've, uh, been in South America for a bit."

I don't engage, not wanting to hear any details of his exciting life elsewhere.

Unlike Erica, I'm not impressed by his bylines or his thousands of social media followers.

While the public eats up his anecdotes and stories, I'm stuck waiting for the call that never arrives.

At least, I used to be.

I refuse to do that any longer.

My father shifts in his seat as he picks an imaginary piece of lint off his sweater. "I just got back into town."

"Okay."

He takes a breath. "And I'll be back here for a while."

I've been too baffled and angered by his sudden appearance to even have speculated as to why it's happening.

And now it's starting to make sense.

"In this country?" I clarify.

He smiles widely. "In this state. This town."

My mind immediately goes to the worst place imaginable. "Why? Did something happen?"

"Yes, but a good something," he says on a laugh.

The fact that he can find humor even while I panic is a perfect example of why I shouldn't reveal any emotions or vulnerabilities to him.

I still haven't replied to his cryptic response, but instead of elaborating further, he only holds up his hand. I don't understand what he's trying to show, do, or prove with the gesture, and I meet his gaze in confusion.

Infuriatingly, he just tilts his head back to his palm and waves his hand.

And then I see it.

He's holding up his *left* hand, and there's a gold band on his ring finger.

"You're married?" I say in disbelief.

"Surprise," he singsongs. "I got married last month."

I'm legitimately too stunned to speak, but he doesn't seem to be done gushing anyway.

"Her name is Nicole, and she's wonderful. Beautiful, smart, driven. She's an American, but she's been living in

Brazil for the past ten years. That's where we met, actually, when I was covering some protests down there, and...we clicked."

"You clicked," I repeat dumbly.

"We've talked a lot about our future, how crazy my schedule is, that sort of thing. It took a bit of coaxing on her part, but I'll be on temporary leave for the next few months, then I'll likely travel at a reduced rate or do something remote." He pauses and runs a hand through his hair. "Or maybe I'll finally get around to writing that book I've been thinking about."

"That is...great." I attempt to snarl the words, but my shock has yet to wear off, so they come out lifelessly.

And, of course, he takes my words at face value.

"I'm so happy to hear you say that," he continues. "Especially with the baby, it's a little more complex."

I blink in confusion. "Wait, what?"

His smile is so wide that on anyone else it would be infectious. "Don't worry, we're going to get a place that's big enough for all of us. I think the baby will stay in our room for the first few months—"

"What are you talking about?" I demand. "What does The Baby have anything to do with this?"

He chuckles. "I think the baby is going to change everything, really. And, well, I think Nicole wanted me to wait until you met her, but I can't help but share the news! She's due in March. I didn't bring any pictures with..."

His excited jabbering doesn't end there, but the ringing in my ears overpowers the sound of his voice.

His appearance alone was enough to make me want to curl up in a ball and hide, so now that he's dropped this news on me, all I can do is dig my fingertips into the desk and focus on my breathing as I try to process everything.

At first, I'm upset as any logical person would be.

And I'm devastated that he thinks I'm the type of person who would be ecstatic by this news.

Then, finally, I get *angry*.

Like, uncharacteristically so, to a level I've never felt before.

"So, you're going to be a good father this time around?" I snap, interrupting him mid-sentence.

His eyes widen in surprise, and the joy immediately falls from his face.

I don't think he knows what to say next—and honestly, I don't either.

As the teenager, *I'm* supposed to be the unreliable one who makes mistakes and gets excited about falling in love. Not my father, whose passing interest in my existence is suddenly renewed when his new wife wants some semblance of a family, and I finally fit in with his plans.

There's so much bitterness on my tongue that I can't swallow it.

I stand immediately, and I'm going to do the most logical and self-preserving thing I can think of—get out of here.

"Violet, I know you're upset that you weren't at the wedding," he says as soon as my palm hits the door handle. "But if you give me a second—"

I turn to look at him. "If you think *that* is why I'm upset, you're only further proving my point."

And with that, I leave.

But it's not a stoic, put-together departure—it's a

complete scramble where I fumble with the door and barely slide on my shoes before I barrel out of the house.

I move at a speed that I think Kara would be proud of as I take off down the street.

I don't stop running until I'm completely out of breath and have a burning cramp in my side. Luckily, this happens when I'm next to the—thankfully empty—park at the edge of our neighborhood.

It's tucked behind a bank of trees, and in the summer, they've provided nice shade for when the twins goad me into sharing the monkey bars with them.

But now, since it's a Saturday in December and the wind is biting, there's no one around.

I pull out my phone, almost hating to disturb the peaceful place with my voice, but I need reassurance.

My finger lingers over Penn's name, but given that I unloaded a lot on him last night and he's currently miles into a woodsy running trail, I continue down the list, then finally hit the call button.

"Miss me?" Kara teases, answering after the first ring.

"Kara." My voice breaks, and her name is barely intelligible.

Her concern is immediate. "What's wrong? What happened?"

The tears fall as I explain, not sparing any detail.

I don't consider my father a disingenuous or mean person, but it's almost baffling that my best friend gets more insight from one sobbing phone call than he has gleaned from my entire life.

"He's not a bad guy," I rasp once I've cried all the tears I have to give at the moment. "I just think he's ignorant of how cruel he is."

"Where are you?" Kara asks. "Let me come over."

My head is already starting to pound from the release of emotion, and I take a deep breath, letting the cool air fill my lungs.

I shake my head, even though she can't see it. "You don't need to come. I'm in the park by my house. I just... wanted to talk."

"I get it," she says.

Because of course she does.

"Thank you," I tell her honestly. "You mean the world to me."

She laughs. "No need to get all mushy on me."

That makes me smile.

"Do you feel better?" Kara asks.

I press my palm against my cheek. "A little."

"Do you want me to beat up your dad for you?"

"Tempting." I chuckle. "Because I think you might actually win in a fistfight."

"Violet?" A familiar but very welcome male voice cuts across the park.

"Is that Ryan?" Kara asks, relief in her voice.

"Yeah," I tell her.

"Good. I don't want you to be alone. Just...please call back if you need me, okay?"

"Okay," I agree. "And thanks."

"Don't thank me," she says adamantly. "It's what I'm here for."

I smile as we end the call just in time for Ryan to sit

beside me and slip his warm winter jacket over my shoulders.

"Thank you," I mumble as I slide my arms into the oversized sleeves.

He ducks his head, gesturing to my phone as I twist it in my hands. "Kara?"

"Yeah."

We sit in silence for a minute, and it feels good just to have him beside me as my breathing works its way back to normal.

"How are you feeling?" Ryan asks quietly.

"I…" I exhale. "I don't even know."

"That's okay," he reassures me.

"Actually, that's a lie," I say suddenly. "I'm *pissed*. And sad. And I think I'm still in shock."

"That is also okay. No one gets to tell you how to feel in this situation. Or any other one. I'm just sorry that you got bombarded with it. Him and the news."

"I just wish…" But then I trail off.

I look up at him and purse my lips, recalling all the times he's done something like this—brought me a different article of clothing when I spilled something on what I was wearing, asked about my day, proofread one of my English papers.

He's proven a thousand times that he's just *there*.

It's almost unfair how wonderful he is.

"You wish?" Ryan prompts.

"That you were my biological father." A fresh round of tears pricks my eyes. "I hate that it's because of me that *he* calls and shows up every few years, just enough to remind everyone that I'm related to him and leave me a total mess. I just wish…I'm glad that I have you."

Ryan reaches over and squeezes my hand. "It's an honor to be your dad, Violet. In any capacity."

I smile as my tears break free and roll down my cheeks.

"I don't know what your father was thinking back then," he murmurs. "And frankly, I'm not sure what he's thinking now just showing up like this. But I am one hundred percent certain he's kicking himself for missing out on so much of your life. He wants to make up for it."

"I don't think I'm ready for all that." I sniffle. "I don't even know if it's something I want."

"The fact you're able to admit that shows how mature you are, Violet. Nothing has to be decided today or even this year."

I nod, accepting his words.

"Now, how about we go home and grab the car?" Ryan suggests. "I'll take you out for a milkshake."

I let him help me up, then he puts his arm around me while we walk back home.

"Sugar really does cure everything," I muse.

He smiles at me. "Truer words have never been spoken."

EIGHTEEN

"You ready?"

Penn asks the question as he skates around in front of me, first backward, then forward, then sideways, and it takes me a second to realize that he's doing this just to show off.

I shake my head at his confidence, wishing my laughter was enough to overcome the unease I feel at the thought of stepping onto the ice myself.

It was Penn's turn to pick our activity, so I should have seen this coming.

To be honest, I was happy to give up the control and responsibility of planning because my mind feels somehow overstuffed and drained at the same time.

But my current trepidation is a good distraction.

Along with the sight of him.

"I can get you a skate trainer, if you want," Penn teases.

He's referring to one of those metal contraptions that

five-year-olds use to hold themselves up while they shuffle along on the ice—clearly, he's trying to rile me up.

And it works.

I stand up immediately and proudly step out, then start gliding.

I'm accustomed to seeing the ice rink during game time when there are plenty of people milling about and the music is pumping, but Penn somehow managed to get access after hours, so it's just us.

Most of the lights are off, and at first, I thought it was spooky, but now that I'm on the ice, I think it lends the arena a romantic and ethereal vibe.

"You're doing great," Penn tells me as I move somewhat unsteadily.

I snort but keep at it.

Kara got me these skates a few years ago for Christmas, and compared to the ankle boots I wore in here, they feel like plaster on my feet. Of course, this is the first time I've actually worn them—and it may be my last.

Penn's skates, by contrast, are a little battered. There's dirt—how, I don't know—caked around the white part that supports the blade, and although the hard material that holds his foot is flawless, I can tell by the easy way he stands that they're perfectly molded on the inside.

If I hadn't been around for Kara's entire skating career, it would be difficult for me to believe that someone could simply practice their way up from my skill level to Penn's.

"Kara's super jealous that you've got me out here, you know," I tell him when I finally feel less wobbly.

"I'm surprised she hasn't converted you into a skater." He glides backward, keeping an eye on me as I move.

"Oh, she's tried. Many times. But it always ends with her lapping me and me falling on my butt, and I don't have the emotional or physical capacity to let her 'train' me anymore."

Penn laughs. "And now? What about with me?"

I know by the excited text messages he sent me this past week and the optimistic, bright-eyed look on his face now that he's hoping this will be a good experience for us.

I think it could be.

"Not bad so far."

"I'll take it," he says. "Do you know how to fall correctly?"

"Grab my knees when I'm going down, be sure not to hit my head, then kneel before I stand again."

"Good."

I wince. "I have more experience in that than I'd like to admit."

On our third lap, I feel comfortable enough to drop my hand, which I'd been holding out toward the wall just in case.

Apparently noticing my progress, Penn turns and slows enough to skate beside me.

I merely glance at him, trying to keep my focus on the rhythm of gliding, but in the brief second our eyes meet, his sparkle with a devilish gleam, and he breaks out into a wide grin.

"Do you trust me?"

I frown. "Potentially."

He chuckles. "Really?"

"Yes, of course."

"Take my hand," he instructs, offering it to me.

I do.

And we spend a lap getting coordinated together, skating in sync.

Once he senses I'm okay with this, he transfers my hand into his other one, like we're promenading around, and slides his free palm around my waist.

I gasp as he turns us backward in a wide arc.

I'm a little shaky, but with his grip and reassuring smile, I find the challenging new motion kind of exhilarating.

My heart pounds in my chest as he leans down to kiss me, and as soon as his lips touch mine, I lose it.

I completely forget what we're doing, and my limbs give out.

I tumble to the ground, taking Penn down with me, and we both apparently forget the rules of falling because we end up tangled together with my face smashed against his chest and his arms pinned.

We both laugh until Penn rolls over and lets out a groan.

"You okay?" I ask as I sit up.

"It's a lot easier to fall with pads on," he says.

The cold is seeping into my jeans, but there's not a chance in frozen-over hell that I'll be able to stand up while on the ice. Thankfully, though, we're only a few feet away from the entrance, so I crawl toward the safety of solid ground.

I right myself before I sit on the edge of a bench, and Penn joins me.

"You can stay out if you want, but I think that's enough for me," I say to him as I unlace my skates.

His brows pinch between his eyes. "Why would I want to go out without you on our date?"

I shrug. "You love it, and I don't know how often you get to do this sort of thing. Skating on empty ice after hours is pretty cool, you know?"

"I do know, and it doesn't happen often." Still, he undoes his skates with rapid precision, moving much faster than me. "But I'd rather spend a whole day on non-slick ground with you than even ten minutes out there alone."

I blink at his words. "That is very...direct. And very kind."

"Nana instilled in me the value of not mincing words, and I think it's important that I tell it like it is. And the same goes for you. I appreciate that you indulged me and went along with this, but you don't have to love it."

"You sure you don't want to be with someone who you have everything in common with?" I ask tentatively.

I don't know why I feel the need to give him a preemptive out, but as soon as I say the words, I wish I could swallow them back down.

Penn smirks. "Where's the fun in that?"

"Is that what you're looking for?" I ask curiously. "Fun? Because I'm not sure I'm the right person for that."

"Honestly? I think I'm fun enough for the both of us."

I elbow his side. "Hey!"

He holds up his hands. "I'm sorry, but it's true. You're smart. And well-spoken. And slightly bossy, but I like it. Also, you're gorgeous. Like, it's great just to look at you."

"Don't butter me up to cancel out all the bad traits," I grumble.

But I'm not immune to his charms.

"I'm just saying true things," he continues. "Those aren't *bad*. They're just accurate, and all of them come together to make you the person you are. And I happen to really like all those things."

"Penn," I sigh.

Before he even catches what I'm doing, I lean over to kiss him.

It's the first time we're unobstructed—no tables between us or chance of falling to the ground—and I'm able to wholly appreciate it.

His fingers slide up from the base of my neck into my hair, and his grasp is just firm enough to pull me in and deepen the kiss. When he parts my lips with his tongue, my entire body melts at how good it feels moving against his.

My heart pounds wildly in my chest, and even though I feel warm, my skin breaks out with goosebumps.

I drop my hands to his muscular thighs, using them for balance as I move even closer, and the contact elicits a low sound in the back of Penn's throat that equal parts stuns and entices me.

He moves from kissing my lips to the corner of my mouth, then down my jaw and onto my neck, which is new and exciting but also kind of weird.

In a good way.

I squirm as his teeth graze my earlobe, and he chuckles in my ear before I pull him back around to me.

And we kiss again.

I have no idea how long this goes on.

Time doesn't exist—I live and breathe by our rhythm as we explore different pressures and touches.

I slide my shaky hands up from his legs to his waist, then glide them over his chest before bringing them to rest on his neck, feeling his erratic pulse.

It's good to know that his body is reacting the same way mine is.

Most anatomy textbooks explain the process of reproduction and how it's accomplished from a biological perspective, but no book or person has prepared me for the way it *feels* to be touched and appreciated.

I could sit like this for hours, reveling in all this newness.

But just as I have that thought, I notice the stiffness in my neck and the way my jaw is tilted up and how my back is twisted in an uncomfortable position.

With no one around to interrupt us, I wonder how long this will go on.

Am I expected to do other things? Do we just keep going like this until we run out of steam or our lips fall off? Will it be awkward to go from *this* back to anything else?

As if he can sense my racing thoughts, Penn presses a chaste kiss to the corner of my mouth and pulls back.

"You okay?" he asks, eyes a little dazed.

I straighten, and the relief is instant, so I give him a nod of reassurance.

He gives me a loopy smile as he runs his fingers through my hair. "There's only one thing that could make this better."

"What's that?"

"Food."

I let out a low laugh. "I should have known. You're *always* hungry."

"Where do you want to go?" Penn asks.

"I thought this was your night to pick," I remind him.

He shrugs. "I don't mind sharing."

"Okay."

We make quick work of putting the guards back on our discarded skates, then slide our shoes back on. As I stand, Penn slings both sets of skates over his shoulder, then puts his arm around my waist.

The gesture is effortless, natural, and that leaves me curious.

"Have you done this whole thing with…anyone else?" I ask him.

"'This whole thing?'" Penn repeats.

"The ice-skating date at an empty rink."

He snorts as he holds open the door for me. "Kind of."

My stomach drops. "Oh?"

"Charlie has made me come with him to try out some moves a few times."

The relief is instant.

"Moves?" I smile as I picture them doing the whole hand-holding and backward skate routine.

Penn waits for me to climb into the passenger seat of his truck before he takes the driver's side.

"Uh-huh." He turns the key, increasing the volume of his words slightly over the sound of the engine. "He went down a rabbit hole on YouTube of ice hockey and ice skater comparisons. And was convinced that he could do it all."

"And you got roped into trying it out?"

"I volunteered for the job," Penn corrects proudly. "I actually learned a lot from trying some footwork and spins, and I swear it's helped me during games."

"That makes sense," I say. "Ryan told me about a football player who took ballet, and it helped him be more limber, even though he was, like, this monster of a defensive player. I suppose the same principles apply?"

Penn nods. "I think so."

"It probably gives you an advantage."

I lean back, getting comfortable in the seat before I turn back to him. "I don't think I've ever heard *why* you play hockey."

"There's not really a big, dramatic 'how I got started' story," Penn admits. "But I should probably come up with one worthy of some ESPN special someday."

I shake my head at his joke, wondering if that will actually happen in his future. "The truth is enough for our conversation now."

Penn smooths his hair and drops his head back on the rest. "My mom always loved it. She played field hockey in college and was a huge fan of the Penguins growing up. She took me to my first game. My dad wasn't as into it as we were, but that didn't stop him from being my biggest fan."

I reach over and squeeze his hand. "That is worthy of an ESPN special. Because it's real."

Penn rubs his thumb against mine and clears his throat. "What about you? Tell me about your parents."

I let out a small laugh. "You've already witnessed the chaos."

"Chaos? That was nothing."

I consider his perspective. "I guess compared to a locker room with almost a dozen teammates it probably seems tame."

"Tell me more," Penn encourages. "Please?"

I smile as I fix my gaze out the front window. "My mom married Ryan when I was a kid, and he's been the best stepdad I could have ever hoped for."

"What about your biological father?"

The timing of this conversation couldn't be worse.

I try to keep my unresolved emotions at bay so I can speak.

"He's not around," I say tersely. "He hasn't been for a while, but now, well, recently, he's been trying to worm his way back in. He's a big, important journalist, so he's spent my entire life traveling and reporting, and Erica thinks he's the greatest person to ever walk the earth. I know it's cool and all, but—"

"But it also kind of sucks?" Penn guesses. "That he's not there for you?"

"Yeah," I say as tears well up in my eyes.

And another truth hits me.

That he's the reason I've been so hesitant—to let go of Erica, to fully give into Penn, to even face everything with him head-on.

Because it's so much easier to block out how I really feel than to open myself up and deal with disappointment or anything else other than the status quo.

Penn presses a kiss against my knuckles as I take deep breaths and try to will the emotion back to where it came from.

I clear my throat. "I think that this is why I've always loved science so much. The clear explanations and rules. The black and white of it all."

"It's much easier than the ambiguity of human emotion," Penn says.

I blink at how wise that statement is.

"Complications can sometimes make it all worth it, though."

I smile softly as I fix my gaze out the windshield, then gasp in surprise. "It's snowing."

"It is." Penn looks at the little flakes with the same sense of wonderment that I do. "But I thought your favorite season is summer?"

I let out a small, bewildered laugh. "You remember that? Well, I do love summer most of all, but who can say bad things about winter with *snow* falling from the sky? And the way everything is quiet outside after a big snowstorm…it's perfection."

My rambling doesn't seem to bother Penn, who only looks at me thoughtfully.

"You know, it's really annoying we don't go to the same school," Penn says. "I want to see you every single day."

"You'd get sick of me," I tell him honestly.

"Nope." He shakes his head. "Seriously, though, after tonight, when can I see you again?"

"Is tomorrow too soon?" I tease, knowing he has plans to go play laser tag with friends.

"How about next weekend?" he suggests. "I have the first playoff game on Friday, but I'm free all Saturday."

"Let me check," I say as I pull out my phone.

After our impromptu grocery shopping night, I've made it a point to actually use my calendar app, so before I agree to Penn's plan, I check to make sure I'm not forgetting any babysitting plans or homework obligations.

I groan at the block of time already marked on my calendar for next weekend. "I have a stupid party to go to."

"How stupid?" Penn asks.

"It's this thing for our broadcast journalism class," I explain. "Every year, the senior anchors throw a holiday party for everyone who helps with the broadcasts."

"Will there be baked goods?"

"I think I'm going to make peanut brittle. And maybe even some white chocolate peppermint cookies. I've also been toying with a way to make hot chocolate cookies that don't taste like s'mores."

"Are you going to keep naming items when I'm already hungry?" Penn asks. "Or are you going to invite me?"

"You'd want to go?" I balk. "It'll be pretty boring. I don't think I lasted an hour last year."

"I'd go anywhere with you," he says seriously.

Cheeks coloring, I smile. "Well, then. Penn Westbrook, will you please do me the honor of accompanying me to a party that I don't even want to go to?"

"Okay, if you insist," he says in false exasperation. "But first, let's go get dinner."

I abruptly realize we've been idling in the car all this time with no destination.

I was so caught up in worrying about what we'd say or talk about or do that I woefully underestimated the connection we'd share by simply being together.

And I'm starting to *really* enjoy it.

NINETEEN

The party is *supposed* to be small.

It's why I only made two dozen cookies and a pan-sized sheet of peanut brittle, but much to my dismay, it's all gone within twenty minutes of being set out. I guess I should be flattered that people are enjoying my contributions, but I'm annoyed there isn't any left for Penn's impending arrival.

Erica, however, is absolutely thrilled with the turnout. She's spent nearly every waking second of the past week texting, talking, or writing about the event, and she doesn't stop until Emily shoves a drink in her hand.

"It's party time," Emily says happily.

I sip on my can of Sprite. "Yay," I say lamely.

"And you're banned from broadcast class talk tonight, Erica," Emily continues. "I don't care if you think our holiday segments this year are the best the school has ever seen. You're done."

Erica rolls her eyes. "You think you'd be more excited, given how great everything turned—"

"No, no, no," Emily inserts. "Be more like Aksa. She's just as involved as you are, but she's *chill* about wrapping up for the year."

"I'm Aksa, and I uphold this ban." She grins. "My house. My rules."

"Fine," Erica sighs.

I lift my drink to cheers Aksa, which she returns with a nod of understanding.

While Emily is happy to follow Erica around like a puppy, Aksa is more forward with her opinions and doesn't shy away from conflict—which I think is only going to continue to be a good thing in her life.

In contrast, I have avoided anything to do with Erica besides planning this party.

Partly because the more I think about her, the more upset I get—I've slowly come to the realization that our friendship might not be worth the effort of the conversation that needs to happen between us to repair it.

After all, we're inching toward winter break, and then we just have one final semester before we're no longer obligated to see each other every single day. And if we have issues keeping up with each other now, I can't imagine how that could improve once we're not in school together.

"There she is," Alex whoops as he joins us.

He, of course, has those same two teammates trailing behind him, and I wonder if there's something inherent in his and Erica's personalities that makes them attract people who exist to be their de facto groupies.

"Are you the reason we have triple the amount of people we invited showing up to my house?" Aksa asks him curtly.

He guffaws. "You guys deserve a big celebration."

"And we brought gifts," one of his teammates says.

In near-unison, Alex and his friends unzip their jackets and pull out full bottles of liquor.

Aksa shifts from annoyance to tentative approval, nodding as they head to the kitchen. "Okay," she calls after them. "But don't spill anything! My parents will kill me."

"They don't know you're having people over?" I ask, surprised.

She smiles sheepishly. "They're out of town for their anniversary, and I only mentioned I *might* have a sleepover with a few classmates."

"Well, this is definitely more than a few."

We both laugh as the doorbell rings.

"So polite," she says as we walk toward the front of the house. "Everyone else has been walking in."

She reaches the knob before I do, and instead of focusing on who is on the other side of the door, I watch as her eyes widen.

"Uh, hi," she says to the newcomer.

I step up beside her, and I feel myself light up as my eyes meet Penn's.

He leans on the doorframe, smiling instantly when he sees me. "Hey, you."

Aksa's head snaps so fast in my direction, I can *hear* it.

"Are you going to let us in or what?" Kara asks, stepping forward with Charlie at her side. "It's freezing out here."

I laugh, then move aside and wave them in.

"Hey, Aksa," Kara says with a smile. "I hope it's okay we crashed the party."

"It's good to see you," Aksa replies as she brings her in for a hug. "It's been forever."

"It really has," Kara agrees before introducing Charlie.

There's a little small talk exchanged that I ignore in favor of grinning up at Penn.

"Nice hat," I tell him, nodding toward the Penguins beanie.

He shoves it in his pocket before he sheds his jacket. "Thanks," he says as he ruffles out his hair. "Jeff got it for me last year for Christmas."

"I kind of like your hair without any covering, though."

"Well, it is my favorite color," Penn says as he leans down to give me a kiss.

Aksa clears her throat just as his lips meet mine.

I blink before I turn, having momentarily forgotten that anyone but us existed in this room.

I suppose it's a somewhat romantic notion, but I'm a little embarrassed. Plus, it's one of the things I hate about Erica and Alex's relationship—their need to shove it in everyone's face—so I try to compose myself.

"Sorry," I say immediately. "Aksa, this is Penn, my boyfriend."

Kara practically jumps up and down at that last word.

"Hi," Aksa says warmly. "Thanks for coming."

"Thank you for having me," Penn says graciously. "But just to be clear, *I* was actually invited, so please don't be mad that these two just decided to tag along."

"But, as we promised you earlier," Charlie says with a huff. "If it wasn't cool for us to join or the party was lame, we'd just go to Sheetz and wait for you guys to ditch."

"Charlie," Kara scolds, smacking his arm.

He glances at Aksa and adds, "No offense."

She laughs. "None taken. These parties can be a toss-up, honestly, but I think things are going well so far."

Charlie nods, then ventures inside and takes a look around. "Nice place you got here."

Somehow, in the weeks I've known him, I have not ceased to be impressed by his massive presence. Now, as I watch him loom over us all and scope out the other party-goers, I recall Penn's anecdote about the ice skating and try to picture it.

"You got *Mario Kart*?" Charlie asks Aksa.

She frowns and shakes her head. "No. I've got drinks, though."

"That'll work," he says brightly.

"Come on," she offers, leading us back to the kitchen. "I'll hook you up."

I follow in their wake and note that it's a little odd to see Penn and Charlie mixed in with the classmates I've gone to school with my whole life, but aside from a few curious glances, no one puts much energy into their presence.

Penn's hand rests on my lower back as we walk, giving me immediate butterflies.

I'm suddenly glad we had that whole discussion about PDA because aside from this and the kiss at the front door, I'm not sure what I'm comfortable with.

But I like this little gesture that's just for us.

More than that, I have the surprising urge to feel his hand on *more* of me, and I allow my mind to wander and imagine what that would be like.

There are all sorts of chemicals and receptors in my

brain giving me conscious signals that feeling him is a good thing, and I want to fully embrace them.

Now's not the time, obviously, and my focus is yanked back to our surroundings by the roar of noise in the kitchen as we enter, which has increased in both occupancy and volume since I was in here last.

We take a few minutes to adjust to this new social situation, relax, make more introductions, and…

"Ah, here." Penn purses his lips as he scours the labels on the selection of beverages, then pulls a can of Sprite and the jug of Hawaiian Punch toward him.

"What are you doing?" I ask.

"I know you're all about recipes and science, but I've got a little experiment of my own," he says proudly.

"Oh really?"

"Yep."

In a cup, he very seriously measures out what he deems to be a proper amount of the light, bubbly liquid, then pours a few drops of the red. Finally, he swirls it together just like I've seen my mom do to a glass of wine.

I laugh as he takes a sip, then squints at the mixture.

"Penn Westbrook, hockey star and beverage connoisseur," I say.

"Lucky for me, I'm only working with two ingredients, so I can't mess it up too badly." He pauses to take another swig. "It's actually really good. Want to try it?"

"I will," Kara cuts in and swipes it from him.

She takes a drink, then nods in approval. "It's good."

"I know," Penn says.

Kara grabs the closest liquor bottle, splashes some into the cup, then stirs the concoction with her finger.

"Thank you, Captain," she says with a wink.

Penn chuckles before grabbing another cup from the stack and making a fresh drink.

"I'll take one of those, too," Charlie says.

Penn grumbles at the request but obliges his friend.

"So, Charlie," I prop my elbows on the counter as I address him. "I hear you're practically an Olympic ice skater?"

He scoffs. "The term is 'ice dancer,' thank you very much. And yes. I've been working on the salchow."

"What is that?" Aksa asks as she drops a few ice cubes into her cup.

"It's a pretty cool move, actually," Charlie tells her. "As you jump, on the ice, of course, you rotate and land on one foot."

"You can do that on hockey skates?" Kara asks. "Or goalie skates?"

"Neither," Charlie admits. "I have to use regular skates. I switch them out for my hockey skates when I'm done practicing my edge work. But I swear it's helped my overall movement."

"Huh," Kara breathes. "That's actually really impressive. Will you show me?"

He snorts. "You think I'm going to give tips to the person who took my starting position?"

Kara rolls her eyes. "So, I should go back in time and remove everything I taught you about having a more effective butterfly position?"

"Fine," Charlie says on a long exhale. "Coach has been talking about utilizing me as a left-wing sub, anyway, which is why I've been working on my actual skating."

"I think it's a great idea," Penn chimes in. "Then you can just barrel straight toward—"

"What the hell are *you* doing here?" Alex's voice cuts through the chatter and laughter.

He stomps right up to us with Erica trailing behind him, and I sigh as I take in the anger that's replaced his normally overzealous expression.

Penn gives me a quick look of surprise.

I immediately realize my mistake—in all the details we've shared, I somehow forgot to give him a heads-up that Alex would be here.

I've just violated one of our 'hard no' rules.

"I'm so sorry," I say quickly.

He gives me a tight smile before he turns back to Alex. "Oh, hey, man," he says, forcing politeness. "It's been a while."

"Since we kicked your ass, you mean?" Alex practically hisses.

Penn bobbles his head as he shrugs. "Wouldn't call a goal on a questionable penalty an ass-kicking."

Alex sneers at him, but Penn doesn't falter.

I glance around for help, intending to ask Charlie to do something as a distraction, but I stop when I take in Kara's expression.

Because it's totally, absurdly *blank*.

She's stepped back from Charlie, almost using his form to shield her while her gaze stays on the ground.

Penn laughs at whatever words Alex just spewed at him, then he puts his arm around my shoulders in a show of ease.

Erica laser-focuses on Penn's palm as he rubs my upper arm, then she meets my gaze with a pinched expression.

"Who's this?" she asks pointedly.

Alex snorts. "The guy with the dumb hair? He's a nobody."

"Dumb?" Penn repeats. "Not a chance. It is *violet,* after all."

Erica visibly jerks back at the realization of what dynamic she hasn't been aware of.

It's not that I purposefully withheld my relationship with Penn to hurt her, but I'm sure she'll take it that way.

However, like the self-assured person she is, she collects herself and steps forward. "Who are you?"

"This is Penn," I offer, waving between the two of them. "Penn, this is my friend Erica who I was telling you about."

"I'm Violet's *best* friend," she asserts.

Kara makes a noise that I can only categorize as a mix of a snort and a choke, which finally reveals her presence to Erica.

"Kara?" Erica breathes. "What are *you* doing here?"

"This party's invitation only and so is the alcohol I brought," Alex spits at the three of them. "You shouldn't be here."

"They absolutely should," Aksa cuts in.

"I thought this was supposed to be a *journalism* party," Alex says venomously.

She lifts an eyebrow at him. "If that's true, then why are you here? This is *my* house, and everyone is *my* guest. I get to decide who stays."

"You know what? You're right. I don't need this." Alex slams down his drink.

Erica, apparently, doesn't have a choice in the matter because Alex puts his arm around her waist and practically hauls her out of the room.

"Oh, what a shame," Aksa says with mock disappointment.

"Cheers to that," Charlie says. "Although, sounds like we'd better savor the drinks while we can."

Kara steps forward, holding out her cup.

Once it's been refilled, she takes a significant drink, wipes her mouth with the back of her hand, then blinks until she looks back to normal.

"Well, that was fun," Penn says.

"You did say you're the fun one," I remind him. "But, really, I am sorry about that."

Penn shakes his head. "It's fine, Violet. I know you weren't exactly thrilled to spend time with him either."

"I'm going to go to the bathroom," Kara announces after polishing off the rest of what's in her cup.

"You want me to go with you?" I ask, a little concerned.

She smiles, then glances briefly at Penn before winking at me. "I'm good."

I don't totally believe her, but sometimes I just need a second to process, too, so I let her go without another word.

"What's Kara's deal?" Aksa asks.

I shake my head. "I don't know."

"I mean, is she single? She dated Melody Richards freshman year, right?"

"Yeah." I steal a glance at Charlie, noting his gaze still sits in the direction Kara disappeared. "But I don't know who she has her eyes on these days."

Aksa smiles brightly. "I'll do some recon when she gets back."

"Go for it," I say with a shrug.

"So, what are your plans for Christmas break?" Aksa asks casually.

"I don't know yet," I answer as Penn mixes another drink. "Normal decorating and watching movies and baking, I suppose. What about you?"

"I think my parents have big plans for us. Lots of family members coming to town from overseas who want to see all the glorious things our town has to offer."

"I've got a few cousins staying with me," Charlie pipes up, finally snapping back to the conversation. "But I'll probably invite myself over to Penn's for Nana's Christmas brunch."

"A Christmas brunch?" Aksa prompts.

And so begins the natural progression of the conversation, starting with food, then moving toward Aksa's role in broadcast journalism until she asks the guys to explain hockey to her.

I chime in here and there, but the longer Kara's gone, the more I start to worry.

"You want to go check on Kara, don't you?" Penn asks me quietly.

"What? How'd you know?"

He smiles. "You've been fidgeting for the past ten minutes. At first, I thought it was because of Alex and me, but I caught on after the third time you looked over your shoulder."

I wince. "Sorry."

"Go," he encourages. "We'll be fine here."

"Thank you." I squeeze his hand and press a quick kiss to his jaw before I slip out.

The two downstairs bathrooms are empty, aside from a few people touching up their makeup, but just as I move to head up the stairs, I catch movement in the slightly darkened office to my right.

The wooden door is propped open, and the light from the hallway shines in enough for me to make out Erica and Kara, who are apparently in the middle of a verbal sparring match.

Their voices are a little muffled, so I can't pick up what they're saying, but I can read their body language. Erica's gesturing wildly with her hands, while Kara stands with her arms across her chest, snapping back at her every few seconds.

As awkward as I feel gawking at them, I feel more guilty trying to eavesdrop—especially when Kara attempts to pull Erica in for a hug and gets shoved back.

Kara holds up her hands in defense.

"What is going on?" I say as I step in.

"Hey, Violet," Kara says as she smooths down her hair.

Erica's still looking at Kara like she wants to scream at her, and I try to diffuse the situation calmly.

"What's going on?" I ask again.

"It's nothing," Kara insists.

"Wow," Erica says, looking hurt.

But it doesn't seem like I walked in on *nothing*, and while I expect secrets and half-truths from Erica, I'm surprised that Kara's keeping quiet about whatever this is.

Kara ignores her and takes a step toward me. "Come on, let's go back to the party."

My gaze flicks between them. "It just seems like whatever I've interrupted—"

"It's fine," Kara says quickly.

"Yeah?" Erica snorts. "What about the promise you made me? The only thing I've ever asked from you? A party is more important than that?"

"What are you talking about?" I demand.

Kara turns to glare at her but softens when she meets her eyes. "You want me to tell her the truth? The whole truth?"

"You're going to end up telling her everything anyway," Erica snaps. "You always do! Both of you *always* choose each other."

I hold up my hands. "Before we unpack those issues, can you please explain this?"

"Erica and I...we had a falling out," Kara says.

"I'm familiar," I say a little sourly. "But both of you have refused to fess up to what happened. Or what the fight was about."

"That's not important," Kara says, choosing to stay cryptic.

Erica's jaw clenches before she straightens her posture and stares me down. "It was about you."

I balk at that. "Really? What did I do?"

"That's exactly it," Erica says in frustration. "You act so innocent and perfect all the time, but you're so judgmental. It's grating as hell."

"Well, that's good to know, I guess." I tuck my hair behind my ears. "So, uh, just to make it clear...this whole dramatic and secret falling out has been about *me*?"

"Yes," Kara says with a frown.

"That's kind of a letdown," I admit.

Kara smiles flatly as she shakes her head. "It seems so trivial now, but at the time, it was so dramatic. Erica wanted to sneak out to see those senior guys. See? Stupid."

"It wasn't stupid," Erica insists. "It was *cool*. And exciting. And you know I had a crush on Dean Patton forever. And they wanted Kara and I to come out."

"Right," I say with a nod. "And not me?"

"Well, they didn't exactly say that, but you would have been all twitchy and weird about it, and I didn't want them to think I was—"

"Shut up," Kara jumps in before turning to me. "Don't listen to her. She's a bad friend, and she's just jealous of you."

Erica scoffs. "Of what?"

"Well, for starters, that she's not dating a total asshole who everyone can't stand," Kara snaps. "I can't believe you're with *Alex Turner* of all people."

"And yet she's the one carrying on some secret relationship," Erica fires back. "She still can do no wrong in your eyes."

"I think I can speak for myself," I say, stepping between them. "Because this all, no offense, seems really ridiculous."

Erica rolls her eyes. "Of course anyone having an opinion that's not yours isn't valid."

"If you've felt this way this whole time, why are we even friends?" I ask her plainly. "It's clear that you don't like me."

"That's bullshit," Erica says. "We've been friends forever."

I shake my head. "Just because we've known each other for a long time doesn't mean that we have to continue something that's not working."

"Come on," Kara says, reaching out for my arm.

"No," Erica interjects, bringing both of our movements to a halt. "You both don't get to walk away from me."

"I think we do." I smile sadly at her. "I think it's been a long time coming, Erica, and I've just been too scared to let go."

Kara squeezes my hand and nods in reassurance.

"I can't believe you're acting like the perfect best friend when you're the one who said she overcompensates for how messy her family is," Erica sputters.

Those words are like a slap in the face.

"You said that?" I ask her as my throat begins to tighten.

Deep down, I'm not that surprised how unfazed I am at the idea of backing away from Erica, but the idea that Kara hasn't lived up to her word absolutely guts me.

"Yes," Kara admits apologetically. "But not in that tone or context. I didn't want to tell you any of this because you don't deserve to hear any of this stuff. I mean, it was one stupid fight that has—"

"No," I interrupt, holding up my hands as I back away.

I can't decide what I'm most upset about in this situation, but I definitely need to get some space.

"I think…I'm maxed out on what I can handle right now," I say.

"Violet," Kara says, stepping toward me. "Let's talk about this."

"Please," I manage. "Don't."

I slam the door shut behind me before I bolt down the hall.

I know she'll simply open it and come after me, but the barrier gives me about a five second head start to dash through the house and collect my belongings.

And just as I turn back into the kitchen, I bump right into Penn.

"Sorry," I say as I snatch up my purse.

"Hey, slow down," he says as he reaches for me. "What happened?"

I don't even realize I'm crying until he uses his thumbs to wipe the tears from my cheeks.

"I'm not feeling well," I choke out.

It's a flimsy excuse, and while he definitely doesn't buy it, he doesn't push.

"Let me take you home," he croons, eyeing me with concern. "I don't think you should drive if you're upset."

I shake him off. "I'm fine."

Penn takes a step toward me. "Violet."

"Penn," I say as confidently as I can. "It's nothing about you. I promise. I just had a big fight with Kara and Erica, and I need to get out of here to be alone for a little while."

"Just…text me when you get home so I know you're safe, please."

"Okay," I say, meeting his eyes. "I'm sorry this night kind of sucked."

He shakes his head as he smiles. "All nights with you are good, Violet."

Oddly enough, that sets off a fresh round of tears before I run off.

TWENTY

I told Penn I wanted peace.

But I don't get it.

My phone, normally a welcome distraction, is a chore. It's been blowing up constantly with Penn checking in and Kara apologizing. I finally had to tell them both I needed some space before I turned it off.

I don't feel like dealing with any of it right now, but I know if I completely fold into myself, my mom and Ryan will push for an explanation. They're already very attuned to me because of the entire fiasco with my father—who I'm also pretending doesn't exist at the moment.

Really, I'm beginning to think that the answer to all the world's problems is to cut off technology and make the biggest batch of waffles anyone has ever seen.

At least, that's what I decide to do.

I let June help me, not making too big of a deal when she overpours the batter multiple times. I even manage to press my lips closed when The Baby drops a handful of cereal into the maple syrup I just finished warming up.

I push all my emotions down, keeping them in check until I'm full from breakfast, then I help Ryan with the dishes.

The warm, soapy water is comforting enough on my hands that I want to stick my whole body in it.

"I think I'm going to go up and take a bath," I say as I wipe my hands.

"But I wanted to take one," Chloe argues.

"Randomly, on a Sunday morning, off-schedule, you want to take a bubble bath, which you notoriously hate?" I deadpan.

She huffs. "Well, I never thought about it until you said it."

"Chloe," my mom says kindly. "How about Violet takes one first, then you can have your turn?"

"No," she yells. "I want to do it *now*."

I don't have the emotional capacity to endure a temper tantrum right now.

"It's fine," I say quickly. "I'll do a face mask first."

"Can I do one with you?" June asks hopefully. "Sister spa party?"

"Not today, June," I say flatly. "I kind of just want to chill."

She deflates. "Okay."

I instantly grimace with guilt. "Maybe next weekend, though."

"Maybe," she says noncommittally before running off to the living room.

"Let me know when you're done with your bath," I tell

Chloe as I go to my room for some solitude.

I get about three seconds of peace before Kevin and The Baby bound in, screaming as they play tag, and Ryan follows, trying to corral them.

After shoving them all out and shutting the door, I collapse on the bed.

I do nothing other than stare at the ceiling and try not to think. It's terribly difficult at first, but eventually, I fall into some tranquil state of nothingness.

"Oh," my mom's voice interrupts. "You're still in here."

I sit up, confused as I take her in, not sure how long I've been out of it. "Why were you coming in?"

"I'm out of hair ties," she says.

I give her a look of skepticism. "And there weren't any in your room or the downstairs bathroom?"

She looks a little sheepish. "I'm sorry. I lied. Sometimes when you're busy, I just like to come in here."

"Why?" I say sharper than I intended.

"Just to have a few minutes in a space that's still yours," she says. "Before I know it, you'll be gone. It's just nice to still feel like I'm involved."

A different version of myself would be warmed by that statement, but I'm exhausted from carrying around everyone else's problems and emotional baggage.

"Is Chloe out of the bath?" I ask instead.

"Yes," she answers. "We're all downstairs about to watch a movie."

"Great," I say, hopeful that means I'll get some peace.

But as soon as I step into the bathroom to clean the toys out of the tub and get ready to relax, I stop short.

The bag of lavender bath salts I use—and that was

barely used last time I checked—is completely empty and lying discarded on the ground. I bend down to look under the sink, thinking maybe I confused that bag with another, but sure enough, the empty one is it.

Even worse, the container of mud mask is sopping wet and ruined, and the basket of all my nail polish is missing.

I have a hunch who is responsible.

Before I go downstairs, I fling open the door to Chloe's room, which she shares with June, and confirm my suspicion that the little monster is to blame.

All my nail polish bottles are scattered on her bed—she, apparently, decided to use them as paint on paper instead of on nails.

But given the amount of actual fingerpaint we have in this house, I'm *furious*.

All the anger, helplessness, and rage that I've been desperately suppressing comes to the surface at once, and I have to bat away angry tears before I storm out of their room.

I go back to my own space, intending to let all my frustration out in private, but as I search for my favorite hoodie to put on as a comfort, I come up short and realize it's not there.

Even worse, I notice a few other little things missing, too.

I bound downstairs, uncaring that the loud thumps of my footfalls echo through the house.

When I step in the living room, the first thing I notice is that Chloe has bunched up the very article of clothing I was looking for to use as a pillow, which means she ransacked my room and specifically pulled this out to claim as her own.

Without a word, I walk over and yank it out from under her.

"Violet," Ryan says in surprise as Chloe yelps.

It's a little harsh, but I'm *mad*.

And I can't stop this from being my outlet.

"How many times do I have to tell you not to go through my stuff?" I yell at Chloe, who immediately starts crying. "You've ruined all my nail polish, and you're stealing my clothes?"

Ryan softens a bit, understanding that this is an ongoing battle, but Mom grimaces.

"We ran out of finger paint, so June asked to borrow some colors for her art project last week," she explains.

I groan. "Seriously?"

"I think I have some extra bottles upstairs," my mom offers.

Her nails are painted a mauve color, which isn't a shade I prefer on myself.

"No," I say a little harshly. "I'll just go without. It's fine."

"I'm sorry," she says.

Kara's words, fed by Erica—about how I'm overcompensating for the chaos of my family—ring in my head, and for just one second, I wish I didn't have to put up with it.

"It's not enough," I tell her.

"Violet," Ryan says, standing up with a confused and annoyed expression on his face that I haven't seen in years.

Chloe's letting out big fake sobs, and I roll my eyes her way—and balk as I notice something else.

"Your hair is completely dry," I say slowly.

She immediately stops with the waterworks and looks up at me with wide eyes.

"You didn't even take a bath, did you?" I snap. "What, did you just dump all my bath salts down the drain or something?"

"Yes," she says proudly. "You were being mean!"

"How the hell was I being mean?" I demand.

"Violet," my mom gasps. "Language."

I close my eyes and take a deep breath before I can say something I will *really* regret.

"Violet, why don't you go out for a bit?" Ryan suggests. "We'll get everything sorted out here. And, Chloe, don't think for a second you're not about to face a massive punishment."

At the sound of her gasping breath and renewed tears, I take his advice before I totally lose it.

Without a second thought, I grab the keys from the hook and head out in the car. The change of surroundings is good, along with the music I put on, and I zoom with no destination in mind.

I don't have my phone or my purse or anything else I need to exist in the real world, but frankly, I don't feel like being part of society right now—I just want comfort.

And I realize the one person capable of helping me feel it right now.

I make a sudden U-turn, earning myself a few honks, and within twenty minutes, I come to a stop in front of Penn's house.

Thankfully, he opens the door himself after I knock, and I immediately fall into his arms.

He catches me without hesitation. "I've been worried about you," he says into my hair.

I pull back and stand on my tiptoes, giving him a quick kiss before he pulls me inside.

"Are you feeling better?" Penn asks as we head up to his room.

"Not really," I admit, collapsing on the bed.

In a different headspace, I would feel *something* about what I've just done, but there's nothing romantic or sensual about my sprawling out on top of his comforter at the moment.

Penn seems to understand this, and he joins me, lying on his side and brushing a few errant strands of hair away from my face.

We lie like that for who knows how long, eyes locked and his fingertips brushing against my hair, then dragging along my arm.

"Actually, I take that back," I say, breaking the silence. "You are making me feel better."

"Good."

I reach for his hand, then hold it against my chest. "I think sometimes it's nice to just *be* in someone's presence."

He licks his bottom lip, seeming unsure about whether to open his mouth, but whatever expression is on my face apparently encourages him to go for it.

"When my parents died, I went through a lot. I mean, I guess that's kind of understating it really, but it's true. Nana and I both mourned, but we clung to each other... but, selfishly, I just kept thinking about how I was worried that I'd just lost two people who loved me unconditionally. And there was no guarantee I'd ever get that again."

I smile at his honesty. "I think someone will someday."

The corner of his mouth ticks up. "I hope so."

I press a kiss to his fingertips.

"But I think Kara's one of those people for you," Penn admits quietly.

I let out a sigh. "In the context of what you went through after your parents, I feel kind of silly for getting so upset."

Penn shakes his head. "Don't. It doesn't matter what the circumstance is...parents dying, parents lying, friends saying things they don't mean. Whatever it is, it all hits us differently. There's no reason to downplay your emotions just because someone else might be going through something."

His words fill me with reassurance and light, and I'm so unbelievably grateful for him.

"I've been feeling crappy ever since my biological father showed up," I whisper.

Penn frowns as he moves a little closer. "Kara gave me some background on that, too. Sorry, it just kind of all spilled out last night."

"It's okay." I let out a breath. "So that's been rough, and I told you a little bit about my issues with Erica, and that was *before* last night happened. And then today, I was trying to keep everything together, to be in a good headspace, but all my siblings were just all over my stuff, and...I don't know. I just got really, really angry and overwhelmed."

"That's logical and normal."

I laugh lowly. "I appreciate your vote of confidence."

"Just telling the truth."

"The worst part is that all this arguing and the annoyances are the result of everyone else and how I have to navigate around them." I pause to renew my grasp on his hands. "I just feel that that's a pattern in my life I didn't realize until recently."

"Pattern?"

"I just feel like I'm always doing things at the whims of other people. Like, I never have anything that's just for me."

The corner of Penn's mouth ticks up. "You're wrong about that."

I eye him skeptically. "What do you mean?"

"I think I'm just for you."

I look at him—*really* look at the sincerity in his eyes—and consider the way he let me drop in on his life.

I've taken what's clearly his preferred spot in the bed and brought my emotions and problems to his doorstep, and I wholeheartedly believe him.

And then I kiss him.

TWENTY-ONE

I'm becoming what I've always hated.

On the first day of Christmas break, I apologize to my siblings for my language and outburst—even though Chloe doesn't deserve it—then knock out a few homework assignments, manage to actually do some self-care, and bake up a frenzy.

After that, I'm free to spend all my time with Penn.

It's easy to get swept up in him, and I don't fight it one bit.

Frankly, although I don't love the idea of being the girl who spends all her time with her boyfriend, I think being with him is slowly and surely the cure for what ails me.

I sit in the stands and mess around on my phone while he skates laps around the ice, practicing long after his official team duties have ended. We go on more dates—to the movies, to the arcade, to dinner, to Books & Beans again. June and I even give him a root touch-up, then he valiantly makes us macaroni and cheese after she and I paint our nails.

After that night I showed up and invited myself into his bed, things changed between us.

Like, we've been existing around the other person, but now, somehow, it feels like we're *together*, moving forward as one unit and exploring the world around us.

It helps distract from the Kara-sized hole in my life—and, I suppose, the Erica one, too, but hers is far less noticeable.

Kara's sent texts and stopped by the house twice, but I was out with Penn both times. Then her remaining free time likely got monopolized by the same extended practices Penn has to attend to prepare for the postseason challenges ahead.

Part of me does wish that my relationship with Kara was just magically repaired. Every day, I'm inching closer to purging her words from my mind, but as I think about them now, I still feel a lingering pain and sadness.

For the moment, I try to ignore those feelings—and it's just as simple as pressing the silence button on my father's incessant phone calls.

Because it's New Year's Eve, and I'm actually *happy* with myself, with Penn, and with my plans for the weekend—so that's what I lean into.

It's my first end-of-year celebration with an actual date, and I'm bouncing with excitement as I do a final touchup of my makeup.

Penn and I skipped exchanging gifts this year in favor of having more cash on hand for our dates, which I find very practical. Especially because when my mom, June, Chloe, and I went to the mall the day after Christmas, I was able to score a designer dress on sale.

And now, as I zip it up and admire myself in the mirror, I'm so glad I found it—even if it burned through the money and gift cards I got in my stocking.

It's a strapless, floor-length dress in the brightest shade of glittery gold. Cinched at the waist, it hugs my curves in a way that makes me feel Old Hollywood glamorous, even if the high slit up the leg isn't exactly from that era.

I've done my hair in loose curls and pinned it on one side, and my mom let me borrow some earrings.

Overall, I'm satisfied with what I see, and I open my bedroom door just as Ryan calls up the stairs.

"Violet! Penn's here for you."

I smile as I begin my descent, gripping the banister to avoid a disastrous slip and fall.

"I want to go," I hear June say with a huff down below.

Penn's laughter hits my ears next, and I can only imagine the adorable look he's giving her.

"Maybe next year," he offers.

As I hit the final step and turn into the foyer, Penn stands from his kneeling position—crouched to be level with June—to take me in.

I stand steady as his eyes roll from head to toe, and everything else around us dissipates as we lock gazes.

It's a movie-worthy moment as he steps forward, holding out his hand with a devilish smile.

I appraise his appearance with awe, trying to burn the mental picture of him and his purple hair and dark gray suit forever in my mind.

"You look...wow."

I beam at him. "You look 'wow,' too."

"Would it be totally embarrassing if I took pictures of you?" my mom asks as she cues up her phone.

"Definitely," I say with a laugh.

"But we'd love it, if you don't mind," Penn adds.

My stomach does somersaults at the reminder that we're a *we*.

"Okay," she says brightly as she steps back. "I'll just take a few. Move closer."

Penn closes the distance between us and slips his arm around my waist, and I smile up at him as I'm pulled flush to his chest.

Mom starts snapping photos that are probably going to be some degree of crooked and poorly lit.

"Can I be in the pictures?" June asks, bouncing on both feet.

Penn holds up his other arm, gesturing for her to occupy the vacant space next to him, and she bounds over.

It's an adorable gesture, but it also opens up the floodgates for my mom and Ryan wanting their turn, and then the rest of my siblings.

I entertain the charade until The Baby and Kevin start wrestling, and as the threat of a dogpile grows, I shove them off.

"That's enough," I cut in.

Penn lets out a low chuckle.

I reach for his hand. "We should get going. I don't want to be late."

"You two are going to have a blast," Ryan says as he holds up my coat.

"Thank you."

I slip it on with his help, then I drag Penn out of the house.

"Happy New Year!" Penn calls over his shoulder.

"You haven't even said that to me yet," I say playfully.

I step gingerly over the patches of snow and ice, and he cranks on the heat as soon as we get into the truck.

Finally, he leans over and plants a big and exaggerated kiss on my lips. "Happy New Year, Violet."

"Happy New Year, Penn," I whisper before kissing him again, much slower and more deliberately this time.

He pulls back and buckles his seatbelt. "We really are going to be late if you keep this up," he says with a laugh.

"Fine," I sigh as I do the same.

"Not that I'm complaining..."

"But it's better not to keep Mary and Jeff waiting."

"Nana *has* impressed upon me the importance of punctuality."

If someone would have told me months ago that I would be genuinely looking forward to a double date with two seventy-year-olds, I would have thought they were insane.

But I am really excited for it.

I spent the last New Year's at home with all my siblings, decorating cupcakes and blowing on kazoos at midnight, but tonight, I'm going out—and I feel very adult for doing so.

Jeff, as a holiday treat, got the four of us tickets to some fancy event. The gesture is more than enough, but it comes complete with a six-course meal, dancing, and a balloon drop at midnight.

Needless to say, it's a major upgrade from my normal plans.

When we arrive, there's even a valet who takes Penn's keys, and another person, dressed in a tuxedo, takes our coats before we wander inside.

The banquet hall is tucked into a hotel, and I assume it's usually used for weddings, but tonight, it looks like a winter wonderland. The walls are covered in lights and silver decorations, and the tables are adorned with white tablecloths, fancy dishware, and beautiful glasses.

We make our way to where Mary and Jeff sit, and they both greet me enthusiastically as we exchange compliments.

"I am surprised they let me through the door," I say as we all take a seat. "They don't know that at my house we regularly use paper towels and plastic plates with Disney characters on them."

Mary howls at that. "Penn had a *Finding Nemo* sippy cup that he took with him everywhere."

"A classic movie."

"And he had a little Dory stuffed animal," she adds.

"Which I still have," Penn says proudly.

"You still sleep with her?" I ask him, tone teasing.

"She lives at the top of my closet," Penn tells me with a chuckle.

"If you can believe it, the first Disney *Cinderella* movie came out the year I was born," Mary tells me.

"Back when dinosaurs roamed the earth," Jeff says.

Mary rolls her eyes. "Well, aren't you Prince Charming?"

I sigh happily as I scan our surroundings. "This really

does feel like some sort of magnificent ball. But I'd prefer your truck to not turn into a pumpkin after midnight."

"I'll see what I can do," Penn says with a wink.

I watch as Jeff and Penn exchange a look I don't understand, but before I can call them out on it, the server approaches. He offers glasses of wine for the older couple and sparkling grape juice for Penn and me.

"Cheers," Jeff says excitedly.

"To a good evening, good wine, and good food," Mary adds.

"I can toast to that," I say.

"Most of it, anyway," Penn says.

And then we're treated—and I mean in every sense of the word—to an immaculate dinner.

It's almost deceiving how small the portions are at the beginning, earning a joke from Mary about going for fast food on the way home, but she's quickly eating her words.

The courses are small, starting with soup that's in a container no bigger than a shot glass, then the meal is built on top of it.

The second course is a deconstructed salad, served on a long piece of romaine lettuce and topped with bleu cheese, bacon, and herbs I don't even recognize.

I start to lose track of where we're at, but the flavors are incredible. We all gush about every single course, not even recovered by the time the next shows up.

When I finally take a bite of dessert, I have to withhold a moan at the soft, delicious flavor of the chocolate mousse paired with a raspberry and whatever crumble is on top.

"I think I could die happy now," Mary says as she puts

her spoon aside. "If this is my last meal on Earth, I'm ready to go."

Jeff lets out a bark of a laugh. "We've got a lot of life to live yet, Mary."

"Another reference to my age?" she volleys back with a raised eyebrow.

I clear my throat. "The life expectancy of women is longer than men, so you two might be the perfect age to do things right."

There's a beat of silence, and I wonder if I've overstepped, leaning in on such a dark topic on such a lovely evening, but the three of them all break out into laughter.

"There you have it," Penn says with a wave of a hand.

Mary shakes her head, covering her smile with her wine glass.

"Well," Jeff says to Penn before standing. "With that in mind, here goes nothing."

Mary looks at him skeptically as he steps around the table. "What are you—"

The question dies on her lips as he drops down to one knee.

My hand goes to my mouth, covering my shock, as he pulls a ring box from his jacket pocket.

Penn reaches over and squeezes my thigh.

"Mary Martin Westbrook," Jeff says.

His words are low and strong, but a wave of emotion hits him—actual tears gather in his eyes.

Given his demeanor, I wouldn't have taken him for a crier, but I think it's sweet.

"It's said that how you start the year is going to be an

indicator of what follows, but I don't believe in all that crap."

Mary lets out a snort of a laugh as a few onlookers turn to watch the proposal unfold.

"It's nice to get all dressed up and fancy and show you off, but it's the everyday with you that I want to make the most of. I love you so much, and I'd be honored if you'd agree to spend the rest of your life, however long we have, together." He pauses to reach for her left hand. "Will you marry me?"

"Of course I will," Mary says plainly. "You big softie."

He slips the ring on her finger, and they kiss as the people around us start clapping.

"Congratulations," Penn says as he moves to shake Jeff's hand. "You're a lucky man."

"Don't I know it," Jeff breathes.

I hug them both, and Mary doesn't shy away from showing off the sizable diamond on her finger.

"It's stunning," I say genuinely.

"Penn helped me pick it out," Jeff says.

Mary chuckles as she embraces her grandson. "I take it that means we have your blessing?"

"Jeff actually asked me for it months ago," Penn explains. "I, of course, told him that I appreciated it, but there's nothing in the world that would stop Nana from doing what she wants."

"You got that right," Mary says, pressing a kiss in his hair.

"Congratulations," the server announces as he presents the couple with a bottle of champagne.

They pop it open as the big band starts up, and the next

hour passes without our moods faltering for even a second. We all clink our glasses together in celebration, then take spins around the dance floor, reveling in it all.

When the song turns slow, Penn holds out his hand for me to take, then twirls me before pulling me against his chest.

"Is that one of Charlie's ice-dancing moves?" I ask good-naturedly as I lock my arms around his neck.

"That's a Penn Westbrook original," he corrects as his palms meet my back.

"Really?"

"Yes. I've never attempted it before now, so I'm trying to play it cool that I pulled it off."

I laugh as we sway to the beat. "You're happy?"

"Definitely." He glances over at Jeff and Mary, who are looking at each other with stars in their eyes. "And, self-ishly, them making it official is helping me feel a lot better about my decision for next year."

"You've finally put an end to the recruitment madness?" I ask.

"Well, I'm going to next week," he says before he lets out a breath. "I've decided on Colgate. At first, I was nervous about the campus being so far away from here, and putting such a long drive between me and Nana, but the program, the facility...everything, really, is great."

I almost choke at those words.

"Besides, I didn't want to start the year hanging in the balance. I mean, this is my future, and it just feels right." He pauses to kiss me. "*Everything* right now feels right."

I nod but still don't make a sound.

Penn eyes my lack of reaction curiously.

I don't blame him—if I were him, I'd be a little affronted by my lack of excitement.

But instead of aimlessly *dating* in high school, there's potential between us now with close proximity next year, and I find it a little daunting.

"You don't think it's the right choice?" Penn asks eventually, apparently interpreting my silence as doubt about his future.

"No, I think it's great," I say quickly. "Good parameters, and I know from what Kara has said that it's a great program."

He blinks at the realization. "Is it crappy that I totally forgot she's going there, too? Especially because…that means you'll be there to visit, right?"

"Assuming things get sorted out between her and me."

"Everything will work out," he says confidently. "You said you applied to a bunch of schools?"

"I think I'll hear back in the next few weeks."

I know I should give him all the details—including that we'll potentially be very close in proximity—but something about that feels heavy, like I'm creating a new set of expectations.

"We've got one minute until the countdown begins," a man announces into a microphone.

I really want to be the person who vows to ring in the New Year with no regrets and have a firm plan moving forward, but as the clock strikes midnight, I'm certain that I have no idea what's in store for the year ahead.

TWENTY-TWO

"And so I think we'll end the segment with the hockey piece," Erica finally finishes her ten-minute spiel as she types the words on her school-issued tablet.

I've kept my mouth shut since school resumed, and it's been surprisingly easy to avoid direct conversations with her.

For one, she's busy with all things Alex, and two, she has hit this semester's workload with an intensity I haven't seen since she won last year's improv competition.

"Are we good on this for now?" Aksa asks somewhat anxiously.

She's itching to get this plan done with because she heard there's a pop quiz in next period's history class, and she wants to review her notes.

Erica nods. "We can regroup next week with everyone's notes and outlines."

"Great," the guy from the sports desk says. "Let's go mess around with the new green screen."

He gets a few laughs, and the majority of the group dissipates, following him into the studio.

This first week back to school this semester has dragged. It's always rough returning after an extended break, but it's been even more tiring this time around.

It's only been a few days since I've seen Penn, but even though we text as often as we can, he's been laser-focused on getting ready for tonight's playoff game, and I've missed him terribly.

Erica clears her throat. "Violet, can we talk for a minute?"

I frown as I tap my fingers on the table's surface, noting that everyone else is either out of earshot or too preoccupied to pay attention to our conversation.

"What's up?" I ask her evenly.

Erica chews on her lip, dragging out the inevitable. "Kara told me about all the stuff with your dad."

That wasn't what I expected her to say.

And if this is her opener for an apology, it's not off to a great start.

"Did she?" I say, tone a little harsh. "You guys are talking now?"

Erica has the audacity to look annoyed. "Is that a problem?"

I shake my head and adjust in my seat to get ready to stand and switch tables. "I don't need this from you."

"Wait," she says, putting her hand on mine.

It's not the gesture that makes me stay put but her grimace.

"She's just worried about you," she explains gently. "And she's kind of distraught that you've blocked her out."

"Yeah, well…" I trail off because I really have no excuse at this point.

"Look, for what it's worth, I'm sorry for everything I said," Erica says quickly. "I guess I never really thought about how all the stuff with your dad might affect you. And the same goes for my treatment of you. Before and after that."

"I appreciate that," I say evenly.

She lets out a breath. "I've thought a lot about it, and Kara was right. I've always been jealous."

"Jealous?" I repeat.

She glances around to make sure no one is listening in. "Even when the three of us were super close, I always kind of felt like the odd person out."

"Well, I'm sorry I ever made you feel like that," I tell her honestly. "It was never my intention."

"Looking back now, I tried to drive a wedge between you, and it shows how much Kara loves you that she told me off and cut all ties."

"She does," I say with a nod.

She swallows before offering me a small smile. "But that aside, I guess I didn't realize how much things have changed between you and me. It kind of hit me the night of the party, though. I hope it's fixable."

"I'm not sure," I admit honestly. "I think I just need some time to let everything cool down."

"That's fair," Erica says, but her disappointment is clear.

"And I still need to patch things up with Kara," I say as a deflection.

"You should," Erica says sternly.

I quirk my brow as a response.

"I think we could all stand to be more direct with one another," Erica says. "I think you're more hurt than you want to let on about what happened between Kara and me, mad she didn't tell you what happened, when really she was protecting you. And then I babbled something stupid that she said. Really, everything is pretty much my fault. And since you no longer look like you want to smack me in the face, why haven't you let her off the hook?"

I open my mouth but close it almost immediately because I can't think of a good answer or retort.

But I do have a solution.

I check the time on my phone, then shove all my belongings in my bag as I stand.

"Where are you going?" Erica asks.

"To fix things with Kara," I say simply as I rifle through the pockets, looking for my golden ticket out of here.

"Now?" Erica balks.

I nod distractedly. "If I leave now, I can make it to their away game."

"You could just call her, you know," Erica reminds me.

"I could," I say, then cheer silently as I pull out the unused hall pass.

I wasn't planning on going to the game tonight because it's about an hour drive from here, but now I have a heightened purpose for going.

"You're cutting class?" Erica asks incredulously as I pull my keys out of my bag.

"Oh, uh, yeah," I say. "I guess I am."

It's commonplace for sports teams to miss a period or two for games, and while I've never gotten the opportunity to do so—having never joined such an activity—today, I'm deciding that a little case of senioritis won't hurt anyone.

I don't think my mom and Ryan will be *that* annoyed—if they even find out.

"Okay," Erica says in slight disbelief.

I turn back to her once more before heading over to our teacher's desk. "Oh, and one last thing. You're doing your own homework from now until we graduate."

"Seriously?"

I nod. "Seriously. Consider it part of the deal of us moving on."

"Got it," she relents.

I half-smile at her, then get moving.

It's almost too easy to flash my hall pass and fake like I'm heading to the library only to slip out the side doors and make a beeline for the parking lot—so the exhilaration of my little rebellion doesn't hit me until I'm officially on the road.

I get turned around twice on the drive, so I'm rushing when I finally arrive at the arena.

I tug on Kara's spare jersey, which is still folded primly in my backseat, as I head inside.

I've never even heard of this school that Greene is playing, and despite it being the semifinals, the support stands are mostly empty for both sides, even though the game is in the final period.

The score is 5-2 in our favor, and yet, even with that result, I know Kara's going to be bummed that she let those two goals get past her.

I find a seat right behind the net, resigned to wait for

either the game to end or for her to turn around and notice me.

I'm not sure which will happen first, but in the meantime, I watch her back.

Literally.

She idles in the net, concentrating on the gameplay and shifting her weight around like she always does. Just the sight of her brings me so much comfort and ease, I want to cry for these past few weeks we've lost.

I know I was too hard on her, but I also know that she'll be quick to forgive.

And I'm not sure I deserve that.

Charlie sees me first and offers me a nod before focusing back on his position. I'm glad to see that his coach followed through on getting him game time.

Penn waves at me as he's taken out of the game with a few minutes left, and Kara turns to see who he's looking at.

I step up to the plexiglass and tap my hand against it. "I'm sorry," I call to her, even though she can't hear it.

She nods at me before the action picks back up, and I try to watch patiently as the clock winds down. Once it does, instead of rushing off toward the locker room like they normally do, Greene's players are caught up in celebrations on the ice.

As they should—this is a big deal for them.

Winning this game means they're advancing to the finals, and along with a trophy, it's a great way to cap the season off.

A reporter from a local news station pulls Penn aside to interview him, and he drags Kara along, not wanting her to miss out on the coverage or the experience.

Once they finish, Kara and Penn head in the direction I've moved to meet them instead of back with their teammates.

"I've got to get you one of my jerseys," Penn sighs, pressing a kiss on my cheek.

I laugh and glance at Kara, whose approach is a little more tentative. "Sorry, but I'm sticking with my favorite player."

"Fine, fine, I get it." Penn waves his hand. "Best friend over boyfriend."

"Hi," Kara says, shy for the first time in her life.

Penn takes this as his cue to leave, and flashing a smile at me, he pushes off backward on the ice, only to pivot and go straight to Charlie to throw his arm around his shoulders in congratulations.

"Kara," I start immediately. "I'm so beyond sorry for everything."

"No," she cuts in. "*I* need to apologize. What I said to Erica was totally out of line and—"

"And totally accurate."

She startles at my easy declaration.

"I definitely do overcompensate for my family and the entire situation with my father. And because of it, I've made some mistakes, like shielding myself from opening up to people and relying on you so much for support."

"As you should," she insists.

"But that's why you deserve better than my silent treatment. I'm so ashamed of how I acted."

Kara moves to the edge of the ice and pulls me in for a hug. "I see the best in you, you know," she says quietly.

I pull back and smile. "I feel the same way about you."

"Yeah?"

"Yeah."

"Are we good?" Kara asks, needing it spelled out.

"More than good," I beam at her. "We're great, and you need to get in on the celebration."

"Will you stick around, though? I think we're doing the whole diner and cookie shenanigans. I want you there. Please."

"That sounds perfect," I tell her.

I watch as she rejoins the team, who all whoop and holler for a few minutes, then I head to the lobby, intending to find a comfortable place to wait for them.

And as I sit down, my phone pings in my pocket with a message from Erica.

Alex won his hockey game.

I find the fact that she sends me a text about her boyfriend after we've just barely reconciled very annoying until I realize what exactly it means.

Alex and his idiots will be up against Penn, Kara, and Charlie's team for the finals.

TWENTY-THREE

"We've decided to elope," Mary says casually as she enters the living room.

Penn and I both jerk up from our cozy spot on the couch.

"What?" he asks. "Like in Vegas?"

Mary sits down on top of the coffee table, facing us, but glances quickly at Jeff, who is pulling the homemade pizzas out of the oven.

"No, no," she says with a laugh. "Could you imagine having Elvis marry us?"

"You could hire an Elvis anyway," I suggest with a grin.

She chuckles. "I guess it's not really eloping if we're announcing it early, but we don't see any reason to hold off. We're going to the courthouse on Valentine's Day."

"That's cool," Penn says enthusiastically.

"And we can get you out of school that day, Penn," Jeff says as he pulls the pizza cutter out of the drawer.

He grins. "Even better."

"A Valentine's Day elopement?" I say. "That's adorable."

"I'm thinking we'll do something low-key, maybe getting hitched in the morning, then have brunch somewhere over the following weekend."

"I'll do whatever you want," Jeff says as he steps into the alcove that separates the two rooms. "But for now, dinner is served."

These little date nights have become a regular thing for us, and tonight, we watched a few YouTube videos—and I read recipes—on preparing our own dough before we made our own individual pizzas.

Jeff and Mary stuck with the classic cheese and pepperoni. I added pineapple to mine—much to Penn's disgust—as well as spinach, while he went all out, adding sausage, peppers, olives, and every other ingredient he could find in the house. Minus pineapple, of course.

Once we've settled in with our plates, Mary turns on a movie.

It's some old-timey black and white film, and I follow along with the plot loosely.

But I'm a little distracted.

While I obviously find their upcoming nuptials charming, it's got me thinking about their dynamic and the other relationships in my life.

Like, for Ryan and my mom, I was around—albeit very young—when they first got together, but I wonder what an added pressure it was for them to date, knowing that I was part of the deal.

I always think of them as an infallible unit, so I've never considered their own love story. But if they met now or in high school or later like Jeff and Mary, how different might they and their circumstances be?

My newfound awareness of these unknowns is making me reflect on how I've treated people in the last few months, making them a part of my own narrative instead of appreciating how they exist in their own.

I think everyone deserves that, though.

Even my biological father.

And that thought doesn't gut me as much as I think it would have once.

I blink as Jeff flicks the lights back on, and I realize I must have zoned out long enough to let the credits roll.

Mary and Jeff make a huge fuss, insisting they be the ones to clean up since Penn and I did most of the prepping and cooking, so he and I are left to our own devices.

"Do you want to play some *Mario Kart*?" Penn asks.

"Actually…I think I want to go talk to my father," I say slowly, testing the idea out loud.

"Really?"

"Yes," I say, gaining more confidence at the thought.

He jumps up immediately. "Okay, let's go, then."

I laugh as I join him, then put a hand on his arm. "I can handle it myself."

He nods as he grabs our jackets from the closet. "Oh, I know you can."

"Thank you," I say, zipping up my coat.

"But I want to be there for you," Penn tells me. "At least let me drive you there? I can wait outside and be available if you need me for anything."

His thoughtfulness never ceases to squeeze my heart.

"That sounds really nice, actually," I admit. "Plus, if it goes south, we can binge cookies after."

Penn smiles and shakes his head. "When it goes *well,* we can still binge cookies."

"It's a deal."

"Nana," he calls. "We're heading out for a bit."

"Okay," she returns. "Drive safe. And don't stay out too late."

"We won't," I answer, even though I can't promise that.

I have no idea what's going to happen—or if my dad is even going to be home—but we go for it.

Ryan gives me the address without pressing *why* I want it, which I'm grateful for, and then Penn and I have a relatively quiet car ride across town—minus the voice of my GPS guiding Penn where to go.

We approach a neighborhood I've never been to before, with a nice array of shops and restaurants, and wind down a street, toward a narrow row of townhouses. There must be two dozen of them, all attached, and I squint at the little numbers on the doors as Penn's truck crawls along.

"That's the one," I point out.

Penn pulls over and glances at me after he throws the car in park. "You ready?"

I take a nice, long, deep breath. "I think so."

"I'll be right here if you need me," he says reassuringly.

"Thank you, Penn. I mean it."

I hop down from his truck and smooth my hair, suddenly wishing I had spent more time on my appearance. My jeans and cozy sweater are a perfect date night outfit, but as I approach the front door that has my father on the other side of it, I decide I probably would have only felt more prepared wearing a suit of armor.

There are white blinds over all the windows, so while I can't see in, I assume that the lights flickering on inside means someone is home.

I press the doorbell, then stand back, heart pounding in my chest as the sound of footsteps picks up.

The door opens, revealing a petite brunette who glances at me curiously.

I expected my father, not this woman whose name I can't recall at the moment.

"Oh, uh, hi," I say, trying to wrack my brain.

She tilts her head in assessment. "Can I help you?"

"I'm—"

I lose my train of thought as she cradles her stomach.

When my father mentioned his new wife and the baby they're expecting, I was so caught up in the shock and disbelief that I didn't absorb the fact that I have another *sibling* on the way.

The experience itself is not new, obviously.

But every time my mom got pregnant, she and Ryan would include me when they went to get their first ultrasound, and they'd build the excitement of how our family was expanding and cement my place as the older sister.

Yet this woman is due to bring another brother or sister of mine into the world, and I don't know anything about her or the baby.

I meet her gaze as her eyes widen.

"You're Violet," she says suddenly.

I clear my throat. "I am."

Before I know what's happening, she throws her arms around me.

It's awkward for her to hug me so fiercely, but she's pinned my arms at my sides, not giving me the chance to reciprocate even if I wanted to.

"It's so wonderful to finally meet you," she gushes before she pulls back. "I'm Nicole. Come in, come in."

I smile tightly as I follow her inside.

"I wasn't sure if your busy school schedule would give us a chance to meet before the baby arrives," she says genuinely.

I quirk a brow at her words, wondering if that was a white lie my dad fed her to explain my absence or if she's just being polite.

"I've actually just boiled some water," Nicole says. "Do you like tea?"

I clear my throat. "Yes. Usually in, like, lattes or whatever. I'm not a coffee person, though. Well, uh, my mom doesn't think it's a good idea for me to have caffeine at my age. Which is kind of wild, given that she works at a coffeeshop. It's not just a coffeeshop, though. It's a bookstore combo, but it's, like, super cozy, and the baked goods are the best. Well, not better than mine most days, but I don't tell anyone that. And, uh, I don't know why I just told you all that."

I stop as soon as I realize I'm nervously rambling, but Nicole looks absolutely thrilled with the information I've just shared with her.

"I'm a total caffeine addict," she says, pulling two mugs out of the cabinet. "Before I got pregnant, I used to have three cups before lunch sometimes. But my doctor has me on all this herbal tea instead, and it's just not the same."

I chuckle at her wistfulness, surprising myself with how immediately I warm to her, then I lean against the counter as I scan the space.

I'm surprised to see several pictures of me—my mom likely sent them—hanging up around the house, along with other touches that make the townhome feel less sterile, despite the white walls and beige carpet. There are little decorations from their travels hanging up or strategically placed around the area.

It's clear that this isn't just a temporary situation—they're making a home together.

My father is putting down roots here because he's really going to stay.

"Here you go." Nicole sets the mugs down on the table before she slowly lowers into a chair and waves for me to join.

I sit beside her and fiddle with the little string on the tea bag.

"Can I get you anything to eat?" she asks.

"No, thank you," I say. "I'm fine with the tea."

"I'm always hungry," she groans before taking a sip. "Well, maybe not me but *she* is."

My eyes widen. "A girl?"

"No," she laughs. "Your dad gets so annoyed when I say that, but I just have this feeling."

I nod. "My mom felt the same way with my sister, June, and she was right."

"What about your other sister?" Nicole asks. "Um—"

"Chloe," I supply. "She was a little more difficult to

pin down because she ended up being twins with my brother, Kevin. We didn't even know that was the case until almost the third trimester. He kept hiding on the scans."

"Oh my gosh, twins." Nicole holds a hand to her stomach. "I'm barely handling the heartburn with one right now. Major props to her."

I like that there's no weirdness or jealousy in talking about my mother or my siblings.

But it's not lost on me that I've had a more genuine conversation with Nicole in ten minutes than I have had with my father in…years?

"Is my father around?" I ask more suddenly than I intend.

"Oh my gosh, total pregnancy brain," she says apologetically. "Of course you want to see him. He actually got home from the gym just before you arrived. He's in the shower, but he should be out any minute."

I had no idea my dad was a *gym* person.

This is one of about a million details I don't know about him.

"Your dad told me you're in your senior year?" Nicole prods.

"Yes, we're officially in the new—"

"Hey, Nicole. Do we have any—" He crosses into the kitchen and stops at the sight of the two of us.

His hair is in complete disarray, something I've never seen before, and it's so shocking how relaxed he looks, it almost hurts.

Because I know everything about my mom—her angry face, how she looks when she's trying not to cry at some commercial, the lines of stress around her eyes—and I've missed out on *eighteen years* of this with my dad.

Nicole breaks the silence. "Violet stopped by to see you."

"I'm glad," he says directly to me. "I'm so glad you're here."

He doesn't make a move, though, even as Nicole slowly stands and makes her way to the fridge.

"Well, I think my chocolate pudding and I are going to watch the new *Queer Eye* episodes," she says, winking at me before she leaves us alone.

My father doesn't miss a beat, immediately crossing the room—probably to make sure I'm not some figment of his imagination.

"I'm so sorry, Violet," he says as he sits across from me.

I trace my fingers along the handle of the mug, waiting for him to continue.

Thankfully, he does.

"I know I haven't been...the best father. Or much of one at all. I was so wrapped up in my own life, my career, and my travels. But once I met Nicole, I understood how off my priorities were. That day I showed up at the house...I was hoping to better explain myself, but I didn't realize until after that it's not what you wanted or needed from me. Then I understood that maybe I haven't really ever been what you wanted or needed. And letting that be okay is probably the worst mistake I could have ever made as a father."

I nod, but I don't open my mouth.

"You're an incredible young woman," he adds. "And it's really no credit to me at all."

I suppress a smile at that admission.

"Your mother and Ryan…well, I'm glad you have them both. I know that you're probably furious with me, and I don't blame you at all, but I guess I'm just hoping that your being here means that you might have room to forgive me? And give me a chance to make things right? And build our new family here?"

I let out a breath. "I think I needed to hear you say all that. I'm definitely still hurt and, honestly, a little mad. But I'd like to…try not to be."

Despite the fact that I'm not exactly glowing at his offer, he visibly relaxes and offers me a small smile. "I would really like that, too."

And for the second time tonight, I'm pulled into an embrace I didn't initiate.

But this time, I give into it completely.

TWENTY-FOUR

"Want some of my hot chocolate?" June offers.

She presses up against my side while attempting to suck marshmallows through two tiny brown straws.

"No, thanks. You enjoy it."

It's a good thing I've declined because no more than five seconds later, Chloe springs onto my lap.

"Your seat is better than mine," she huffs.

"It's one row in front of yours," I argue.

She ignores me as she digs her heels into my shin, trying to press upward like that will give her a more direct view of the ice.

"Okay, that's enough." I hook my hands under her arms to roll her off my lap and onto the bench beside me. "You're done."

"Violet," she whines.

"Chloe," my mom says with a sigh as she holds out her arms. "Come here and leave Violet alone."

My youngest sister sticks her tongue out at me as she wiggles herself between my mom and Ryan.

Surprisingly enough, The Baby and Kevin are glued to the game—and they were the ones I was the most nervous to have attending.

Truth be told, I'm not sure either of them understands what is happening.

But they're infatuated enough with Penn and all the noise and movement that they've sat the most still I've ever seen them.

Mary and Jeff sit on the other side of June, and Emily, Aksa, and Erica sit in front of me—choosing the neutral section with the parents and families instead of the student section.

And I, for one, am comfortably warm in Penn's jersey because June asked for the honor of wearing Kara's.

"This is so cool," June says wistfully.

I smile at her before I focus back on the game.

It's oddly reminiscent of the one they played last time in terms of intensity. It's kind of a brutal back and forth with both teams playing viciously and aggressively, no doubt sharing the dream of hoisting that trophy up at the end.

I'm getting light-headed from how often I hold my breath in anticipation.

Between Penn dashing down the ice while stickhandling the puck, Charlie using his strength and size to steal from the other team, and Kara contorting into unnatural positions to block shots, it's a lot to handle.

One would think I'd be used to it by now, but I can

legitimately *feel* the pressure that all the players are putting on themselves.

For a while now, I've compared and contrasted Alex to Penn, and the relationships Erica and I have with them, stacking them up against each other for no reason other than the reassurance that I'm dating an absolutely amazing guy.

But seeing their different playing styles in such close proximity again is fascinating.

And so indicative of their personalities.

Alex is all brute force and no finesse, skating up and down the ice, always toeing the line between aggression and taking penalties—and when he rightfully earns them, he acts like the world is out to get him. Plus, he's a selfish player, choosing to go for the impossible shots rather than give up his chance at glory for a safer bet from one of his teammates.

Penn, on the other hand, despite his talent and affinity for goal-scoring, is a team player. He sets his players up for success, not slacking on defense, and moves around like he's a conductor cueing an orchestra.

Even though he's comfortable in the background, it's obvious he's a star. It's like he has eyes on the entire rink, easily lobbing passes to teammates and putting himself in position to be open when the time is right.

With one minute left in the game, the score stands 2-1.

Penn scored one of those goals and assisted the other, while Alex is responsible for his team's sole point. All of Greene's fans are stomping their feet, drumming up excitement for the potential of the win, but I'm not going to get my hopes up just yet.

Mary leans forward and pats my shoulder reassuringly. "We've got this," she says, full of confidence.

I smile at her before I turn back.

Because she's right—unless something absolutely insane happens, we're going to win this thing.

It'll be great for the team and for Penn's school district, but more than that, I think about the impact it will have on Kara.

The story of her struggle to earn the right to play, then to become the starting goalie for the entire season when they win the district final would be incredible, and I want that for her more than I've wanted anything in my entire life.

Everyone in the crowd, including my oddly paired group, stands when the clock hits the thirty-second mark.

The players on the bench whoop and beat their sticks against the boards, which makes everything feel more charged and alive.

With this lead, Penn could try to drag out the minutes and wait for the clock to wind down, but he's playing with the same ferocity he has since the first second of the game —and so is Alex.

It's why Alex nails Penn with a hit I'm surprised isn't called, which earns him control of the puck.

Alex thrashes forward as all the players converge around him, trying to stop him from crossing center ice. He's moving fast, but Charlie is faster—and bigger—and hits him with a shoulder that veers him slightly off-course.

But it's not enough.

Alex maintains control and makes a last-ditch effort to reach the goal.

I watch in amusement as Charlie does a graceful, well-practiced spin move that confuses Alex just long enough to throw off his aim.

Kara has been constantly adjusting her position in the net, trying to anticipate where he's going to shoot, and when Alex finally does, it snaps forward.

Right into Kara's open glove.

As the final buzzer sounds, she holds up her hand, and the arena erupts in cheers as she gets tackled by her teammates on the ice. The crowd screams, and the team is elated, jumping out of the box and skating toward the growing dogpile to celebrate the victory.

They did it.

They *really* did it.

My siblings, like everyone else, are losing their minds, and my mother, Ryan, Mary, and Jeff all share congratulatory high fives. June and I rush toward the plexiglass and pound on it in excitement.

Kara rips off her mask and skates over to us, smile as wide as I've ever seen it.

"You did it!" I scream.

"We did," she yells back.

"We did!" June adds.

Kara winks at June before she tosses the puck up over the boards, and, surprisingly, my sister catches it easily before she holds it up and jumps up and down.

Penn waves at us before his coach calls for everyone to line up and offer post-game handshakes—and, in my boyfriend's case, interviews—before the trophy ceremony begins.

The ice is crowded with players, coaches, referees,

district employees, and media, but I keep my eyes on Penn, watching as he navigates the crowd.

In a very sportsmanlike move, he glides over to Alex and says words I can't hear before offering his palm to shake.

Alex smiles at him, and at first, it's that charming one I've seen hundreds of times.

Then it quickly flashes into pure venom, and Alex surges forward and sucker punches Penn, sending him stumbling backward to land flat on the ice.

I gasp as the altercation quickly turns into an all-out brawl.

"Hockey is awesome!" Kevin yells.

I crane my neck as bodies swarm and converge, but Penn quickly jumps up to try and stop the retaliation. Even from my vantage point, though, I can see the pain and surprise on his features as he cradles his cheek.

The seconds tick by, and the coaches and referees prove increasingly successful in breaking up the fighters.

I let out a breath of relief—until I see Alex sneer something at Kara.

Witnessing her flinch, I'm infuriated, wishing I was there to jump in.

Fortunately, Charlie steps forward in her defense, but Kara doesn't need his help—she can handle Alex just fine on her own.

And that's never been more clear than when she uses all her force to drive her fist into his face.

There's a collective gasp in the stands as blood immediately gushes down Alex's features.

"I think she broke his nose," Mary says, slightly awed.

"Yeah she did," June says proudly.

Erica lets out a shriek—though on behalf of whom, I'm not sure—as the teams rally around their players.

It takes a full ten minutes for everything to go back to normal, but then the ceremony commences.

I might be the only person laser-focused on Kara's bruised knuckles and Penn's rapidly forming black eye as they finally hoist the trophy in the air.

TWENTY-FIVE

It's a beautiful wedding.

And it's not at city hall, like Mary suggested, because Jeff talked her into having a backyard ceremony on their patio, complete with a tent, heat lamps, and lanterns, so with the snow falling around us, it feels like we're inside a snow globe.

I much prefer this to having brunch at a restaurant that's decorated with cheesy Valentine's Day decor.

Though I guess I don't have much to compare it to because I barely remember my mom and Ryan's wedding, and I've never actually had a Valentine's Day date until this year.

I think having these events happen simultaneously might have ruined me for a while.

But I'm happy about it.

My entire family, and Kara, Charlie, a few of Penn's other friends, an assortment of friends of Mary and Jeff's, and some of Jeff's coworkers are here. Aside from the people I've just met, almost everyone I love is in one place —including my father and Nicole, who looks like she's about to pop at any second.

I smile at the sight of everyone crowding around the dessert table, trying to decide what cupcake flavor they want, as Penn spins me around the dance floor.

I press a gentle kiss to his cheekbone, which is still slightly bruised from the championship game, before I tangle my fingers in the hair at the nape of his neck.

I offered to dye his hair back to his normal shade for the pictures, but Mary insisted he keep it just the way it is.

"This is the best," Penn says quietly.

"It is a beautiful wedding," I tell him, glancing over to watch Jeff twirl Mary around.

"Not just that. I mean, I am happy for them, but it's nice to have everyone in one place."

"I know what you mean."

"Although, you better watch out because June's just waiting for the moment she can cut in," Penn warns me.

I laugh, knowing he's absolutely right. "Making me compete for your affection so close to Valentine's Day? Some boyfriend."

He squeezes my waist, causing me to jump and let out a giggle. "When it comes to you, Violet, there's no competition in the world."

"Say this to me again when you're playing *Ocarina of Time*," I tease.

"That's between Link and me," he jokes.

I shake my head as the song changes.

"But seriously, Violet," Penn pulls back to look me directly in the eyes. "You're the one for me."

My stomach gets all fluttery at his words.

Penn is nothing if not a romantic, which means I'm a little behind in declarations, but I think I have something that will help show him that I'm in this for the long haul.

"I have a Valentine's Day gift for you," I tell him slyly.

"We agreed on no gifts, though."

"I know. But this one is free. Well, not *free*, given that I'm about to be on the hook for a *lot* of money that my scholarship doesn't cover, but Ryan, my mom, and my father have already spoken to financial aid, and it looks like I'm going to be just—"

"Violet," Penn interrupts kindly. "What are you talking about?"

I let out a breath. "I'm going to Cornell. I got into the program I wanted, and I just officially accepted yesterday."

His eyes widen. "Really?"

I nod. "It's always been my first choice."

"Why didn't you say anything?" Penn asks.

"Because it's only an hour and a half from Colgate."

Penn's smile widens to a new depth. "No way."

I stop moving, but I keep my hands locked around his shoulders. "I'm not asking for anything. Like, no pressure. I know we kind of fell into this, so we don't have to be one of those—"

He cuts off my nervous babbling with a kiss, catching my words in his mouth, and each movement he makes is a reassurance. One of his hands pushes against my back, urging me toward him, as the other slides up into my hair, holding me steady.

Penn pulls back too soon in my opinion, but given that

my siblings are making annoying kissy noises a few feet away, it's probably the right timing.

"Does that mean you're okay with this?" I ask him. "Excited? Happy?"

"Those words don't even begin to explain how I feel about you," Penn says seriously.

"Is it *intense*?" I tease as I brush away a strand of violet hair from his cheek.

"Absolutely."

TWENTY-SIX

One Year Later

There's actually more of everything than I thought there would be—press, people, and a general sense of frenzy that tops any of the games I've ever been to before.

I suppose it makes sense, given that this is not only the NCAA Semifinals but it's also going to be broadcast on ESPN.

And I have to pinch myself just a little bit.

"She got us good seats," Penn says, slinging his arm around my shoulders as we settle in. "Better than the ones I had you two in for Regionals."

He's joking through the pain of the devastating loss his team underwent last week, but I'm grateful that he's just as excited as I am to watch Kara's team dominate yet another round as they make their way to the Finals.

Despite that we're hours from where we grew up,

merely sitting in this rink with Penn's familiarity feels like home—and I've been happy to find this feeling again and again with him.

College—hell, this past year—has been incredible for us.

Not just as a couple but as two individual people who are figuring out adulthood and dorm life and everything else. It's been good to build our own separate friend groups and experiences at our own colleges, but I'm grateful that we get to see each other a few times a month.

In fact, the distance from the drama and people we have waiting for us back home has been a good thing in some ways—especially setting healthy boundaries with my family, including my biological father, Nicole, and my new baby sister—but Nana and Jeff do miss us terribly.

Thankfully for them, we got lots of quality time in over Christmas break, and we're already trying to decide how we want to spend spring break, which will be here before we know it.

For now, though, I'm taking Penn's advice, like I've done so many times, and living in the moment and appreciating every single day.

"There she is," Penn says suddenly as the players skate out to do their warmups.

Kara has complained that Penn and I dyeing our hair back to normal—during one of our "sister spa party" sessions with June—has made it more difficult for her to spot us in the stands.

But we are both wearing her jersey for a show of moral support, even if she hasn't seen us yet.

I let out a breath of excitement at the sight of her

smiling at her teammates. "I take that as a good sign of confidence."

"As you should," Penn says. "They're about to stomp the other team."

I reach my hand over to tangle my fingers in his, and our bodies adjust naturally to fit together even with the armrest between us.

I love that he believes in her as much as I do—and that he always has. Actually, it's one of about one thousand things I've grown to love about him, and if there's one thing *I* am confident in, it's that I'm sure to find even more over time.

I tilt my head to press a kiss on his jaw.

He gives me that Penn smile—the one with the lines around his eyes and the sideways movement of his cupid's bow—that still gives me butterflies.

"What's that for?"

I shake my head as I smile. "I just...love you a lot."

He brushes his fingertips over my cheekbone before he kisses me on the lips. "I love you, too, Violet."

"Remember when I had that breakdown in your bedroom? Back when Kara and I were fighting last year?"

He nods. "Of course."

"You were talking about how you were worried about how you'd never be on the receiving end of unconditional love." I drop my gaze briefly, looking at our grasped hands. "I just want you to know that's what I feel for you."

"I know," he says with a smile. "Because I feel it, too."

FREE GIFT FOR YOU!

Want to make your book an autographed copy? Head over to Jennifer's website and get a free bookplate!

https://www.jenniferannshore.com/bookplate

CONNECT WITH JENNIFER

Hi there,

I cannot thank you enough for reading my work. Truly, it means the world to me!

I'd love to connect with you on social media if you're up for it. I'm on all the major social channels, including TikTok (@jenniferannshore) and Instagram (@shorely).

And don't forget to subscribe to my email newsletter (jenniferannshore.com/newsletter) for bonus scenes, new release announcements, giveaways, and more.

All my love! —Jennifer

ACKNOWLEDGMENTS

It's such a joy for me to write this section because with each book I publish, the community of readers, reviewers, and lovely humans who support me grows—and I'm so very grateful.

That said, there are a few people who I want to call out specifically here, as this book wouldn't have come together in its current form without their help and guidance and creativity.

As always, my assembled editing team (I'd love to make some sort of *Avengers* joke here but haven't seen the movie) who help shape the story and these characters: Jen McDonnell, Denise Leora-Madre, Emily Wright, and Lindsay Hallowell.

Next, from a visual perspective, Kelly Lipovich is a true genius in creating such beautiful covers—that are WORTH judging this book by—and Rachel Kilroy is a magnificent human for taking such amazing photos and videos of them to help promote.

I'm so grateful to Kiki and the team at The Next Step PR for helping spread the word about this book—and for keeping my sanity and dates in check.

Also, my review/ARC team, you all are angels who bring the biggest smiles to my face. I'm beyond grateful for the time and kind words and social posts you all put into the world.

Of course, I need to thank my friends and family who have been the best cheerleaders in the world. So much love for all of you.

And, finally, to Morgan Blank, thank you so much for being a wonderful friend to me—and for lending your badass hockey knowledge to this story. I definitely borrowed your tenacity, kindness, and general awesomeness to create Kara's character, and I'm so lucky to have you in my life!

ABOUT THE AUTHOR

Jennifer Ann Shore is an award-winning, bestselling author based in Seattle, Washington.

She writes romance stories that go a little deeper than the standard tropes. Her lineup of more than a dozen books includes standalones, a dystopian series, and a vampire series—with titles such as "Perfect Little Flaws," "Young at Midnight," and "Metallic Red."

Prior to publishing, she led an impressive career in New York, first as a journalist and then as a marketing executive, gaining recognition for her work from companies such as Hearst and SIIA.

Be sure to sign up for her newsletter on her website (https://www.jenniferannshore.com) and follow her on Twitter (@JenniferAShore), Instagram (@shorely), and TikTok (@jenniferannshore).